PEACE & CONFLICT SERIES

I0634442

PEACE AND CONFLICT SERIES
RON MILAM, GENERAL EDITOR

Also in the series:

Admirals Under Fire: The US Navy and the Vietnam War
by Edward J. Marolda

The Air War in Vietnam
by Michael E. Weaver

Capturing Skunk Alpha: A Barrio Sailor's Journey in Vietnam
by Raúl Herrera

Charging a Tyrant: The Arraignment of Saddam Hussein
by Greg Slavonic

Crooked Bamboo: A Memoir from Inside the Diem Regime
by Nguyen Thai, edited by Justin Simundson

Girls Don't: A Woman's War in Vietnam
by Inette Miller

Rain in Our Hearts: Alpha Company in the Vietnam War
by James Allen Logue and Gary D. Ford

MEMORIAL DAYS

VIỆT NAM
STORIES
1973–2022

WAYNE KARLIN

TEXAS TECH UNIVERSITY PRESS

This book is typeset in EB Garamond. The paper used in this book meets the minimum requirements of ANSI/NISO Z39.48-1992 (R1997). ⊗

Designed by Hannah Gaskamp; cover design by Hannah Gaskamp
Cover image from a photograph by Nguyễn Thanh Phú, Project RENEW, Việt Nam

Library of Congress Cataloging-in-Publication Data

Names: Karlin, Wayne, 1945– author. Title: Memorial Days: Viet Nam Stories, 1973–2022 / Wayne Karlin. Other titles: Viet Nam Stories, 1973–2022. Description: Lubbock, Texas: Texas Tech University Press, 2023. | Series: Peace and Conflict | Summary: "A retrospective collection of one veteran's fifty years of Vietnam stories."—Provided by publisher.
Identifiers: LCCN 2022053273 (print) | LCCN 2022053274 (ebook) | ISBN 978-1-68283-179-3 (paperback) | ISBN 978-1-68283-180-9 (ebook) |
Subjects: LCSH: Vietnam War, 1961–1975—Personal narratives, American. | Vietnam War, 1961–1975—Veterans. | Vietnam War, 1961–1975—United States. |
Classification: LCC DS559.5 .K354 2023 (print) | LCC DS559.5 (ebook) | DDC 959.704/3373—dc23/eng/20230111
LC record available at https://lccn.loc.gov/2022053273
LC ebook record available at https://lccn.loc.gov/2022053274

23 24 25 26 27 28 29 30 31 / 9 8 7 6 5 4 3 2 1

Texas Tech University Press
Box 41037
Lubbock, Texas 79409-1037 USA
800.832.4042
ttup@ttu.edu
www.ttupress.org

For my editor, Travis Snyder, for having the literary vision
to include fiction in the Texas Tech University Press lineup;
for my agent, Julie Stevenson, for her faith in my writing; for
Nguyễn Phan Quế Mai, for her friendship and encouragement;
and for Basil T. Paquet, who first gave me the confidence to put
my stories out into the world.

In memoriam, always: Ohnmar Thein Karlin.

Lance Corporal James Stanley Bernard Childers, USMC
Sergeant John Borman, USMC, LL.D

CONTENTS

AUTHOR'S NOTE / IX

LIZARD WINE / 3

MEDEVAC / 23

THE LAST VC / 27

THE VIETNAMESE ELECTIONS / 35

THAT MINUTE / 39

THE WAR ON TERROR / 45

AMERICAN GRASS / 63

EXTRACT / 73

THE AMERICAN READER / 81

MORATORIUM / 91

THE SERPENT / 101

THE TWENTY-FIFTH PLATOON / 113

NESTING / 129

OUR FATHERS' WARS / 149

SEARCH AND DESTROY / 167

MEMORIAL DAYS / 171

PREVIOUS PUBLICATION VENUES / 183

AUTHOR'S NOTE

THE IDEA FOR THIS LITERARY RETROSPECTIVE CAME to me as the result of another kind of out-of-control "retrospective" in the form of thoughts, emotions, images, and dreams I had thought safely lidded in the box of my past: I had written about all that; therefore, it should be over. When I came back from the Vietnam War, over fifty years ago, I began writing because I thought I'd be good at it and because I didn't want to talk about the war and because I felt I owed it to the dead and to the living who might become the next dead. And also because it was, as all writing is, an attempt to control, to impose a grid of narrative and meaning on the uncontrollable.

Over the last two years, perhaps because of the grief of other losses, perhaps because of my age, perhaps because of the age itself which has kept trotting out versions of my war identical in all ways except for time and geography, it all began leaking out of that box and I had to learn again the old lesson that some things are never over.

Hence these stories.

They cover the arc of my writing life from just after the Vietnam War to the present, at least that portion of my work that touched upon war and its seductions and damages. They move, though not placed chronologically, from earlier stories set in the Vietnam War to stories that reflect on the way that war has moved into the lives of subsequent generations, including those caught up in new wars in which the Vietnam experience still resonates. A number of them ended up as parts or chapters in several of my books, but all were initially published as short stories in magazines or journals or anthologies. Several have been somewhat revised or edited from their original versions. There is one school of thought that stories in a retrospective should appear as they were first published. On the other hand, I've never published work that I haven't looked at later and not wished that I could revise, a little or a lot. Putting together this collection gave me that chance, and I took it. For better or worse. And if one purpose of a retrospective is to reveal the way a writer's work evolves over decades, then changes in individual stories can also measure that same kind of growth.

I've been made conscious over the last few decades of not using the word "Vietnam" to mean the same thing as The Vietnam War, as if a war is all that country and culture could or would ever be. And so it is that the word "stories" in the title is not preceded by the word "war" and the word "Việt Nam" uses the correct Vietnamese spelling while elsewhere it is rendered in the American usage. Some of the stories, those I wrote just after I came back, are set in the Vietnam War, but others are about Việt Nam-the-country, as I've come to know it, and sometimes about the ways the old war has continued to ripple into that country and our own and into generations not yet born while it had raged.

At first I thought of presenting the stories in the chronological order of publication, or rooted in the context of the events depicted (for the convenience of anyone who prefers, the previous publication venues list at the book's end is ordered by the date each story was published). But orderly chronology in and after a war is a lie. "Billy Pilgrim has become unstuck in time," wrote Kurt Vonnegut, who knew: that sentence is one of the truest descriptors one can find about the nightmarish quality of traumatic memory. These stories are unstuck in time. A girl in Maryland runs away from Civil War reenactors she imagines to be American soldiers in Việt Nam, while a woman in Việt Nam hides in the jungle from an American helicopter and another tries to extract and then rebury remnants of the war from the earth and from her mind. A man mourns a friend lost in Iraq while a helicopter crewman in Quảng

Trị loads the broken and dead into his aircraft. Extras playing soldiers in a contemporary war film model themselves after older war films while a Marine in the war sees himself as a movie character. A snake coiled around the collective control of a helicopter in Vietnam-the-war uncoils in a soldier come home from Iraq-the-war. The chronology is the chronology of dreams or nightmares or, if you will, flashbacks: images and incidents triggering other images and incidents in a sequence that seems to make no sense—which is exactly the sense it makes.

MEMORIAL DAYS

LIZARD WINE

A RED BANNER WITH YELLOW SLOGANS ON IT FLOATED above the trees near a billboard depicting Hồ Chí Minh leading the people. Donald Barnes, the Missing in Action/Remains Team leader, pointed at another billboard pasted with advertisements in English for condo sales, a tennis club at Hanoi's West Lake. "Makes you wonder what that was all about, don't it?" Barnes nudged Brian. "All that shouting and shooting and running about we did. Isn't that right, Comrade Cam?"

Đào Thị Cam, the interpreter, shrugged, said nothing.

Brian rolled down the window. Bicycles and scooters swarmed the car, their horns beeping constantly. The air smelled of mold and old stone and charcoal and gasoline. A taste of bile came into his mouth, like the memory of fear. Vietnam enveloped him again. The Celica passed into a maze of narrow, dusty, tree-shaded streets clogged with vehicles and people, a jumble in his eyes of stalls hung thick with utensils or clothing, rusting iron balconies, crumbling tile roofs, stained cement walls, buildings pressing tightly against each other, every inch taken, used. Cone-hatted women squatted on the sidewalks, cooking skewers of meat over glowing braziers, the charcoal smoke twisting up into the air. Boxed television sets, CDs and VCRs were stacked high in front of some shops, the parts of a motor scooter laid out, dissected, on the sidewalk. Through a cave-like door he saw a row of young men sitting on stools in front of screens, playing kick, punch and dismember video games, their thumbs dancing over the control pads in their hands.

A building was being torn down on the next block. "Hanoi Hilton," Barnes nodded, tapping his shoulder. Brian had heard a luxury hotel, though not a Hilton, was being built over the famous prison, and he wondered if Barnes had just picked this site to gauge his reaction; the bald, silver-bearded man was grinning at him goatishly. There seemed to be buildings being dismembered on every street they passed anyway, a deconstruction of the city that freed a stinging white dust; it clung to the leaves of the trees, the sidewalks and walls, to Brian's skin now, like the stubborn past. He looked at Đào Thị Cam; she was staring out of the window also. Barnes had told him she was a People's Army veteran; he wondered if she in any way shared his feelings, still saw her city filtered through the dust of the war. But she remained silent.

They parked on a street lined with noodle soup shops. A beggar approached Brian as soon as he left the car, a wizened old lady, her teeth stained with betel nut, her hand extended. Cam put some đồng in it. It was dusk now and cold; the breaths of the patrons wove white wisps into the steam from the bowls of phở.

The restaurant Barnes led them into was upstairs and upscale, with French impressionist prints on the wall, white linen tablecloths, sleek waiters in white jackets. A small plastic Christmas tree, festooned with bulbs, stood on one table; Brian remembered, startled, that it was two days before the holiday. "We're a little early," Barnes said, sitting at a table. Cam sat at the opposite end, nodded slightly to Brian, then closed her eyes, raised two fingers as if to make a point, and rubbed at her temples.

"You're a quiet man, Schulman," Barnes said. "You deep in throes of nostalgia? Having the obligatory flashback?"

"Don's just jealous because he never had a flashback of his own," a tall young man said, walking in, nodding to Brian, and then shaking his hand. He had a cropped, white sidewalls haircut and a pressed denim shirt and pressed jeans and might as well have been in uniform. "He feels unfairly denied."

"The young Captain Wilkes," Barnes said. "Merry Christmas, young captain."

"Welcome to Vietnam," Wilkes said.

"A phrase I'll say he's heard before." Barnes winked at Brian. "This, young captain, is Dr. Brian Schulman. Doctor. If this was a squad, we'd call him 'Doc.' Doc's gonna make his bones for us, that right, Doc?"

"That's a phrase I don't understand," Miss Cam said, opening her eyes. "What does it mean, making his bones?"

Wilkes said something in Vietnamese to her. She seemed not to hear it.

"We're an enigmatic people, us Occidentals," Barnes said. "It's an old Mafia saying, Miss Cam. Means, have you killed someone for the godfather yet?"

"We kill nobody. We're a team for reconciliation," she said bitterly.

"I meant it ironically, Miss Cam. Bones. As in, what we hunt for. We're an ironic and enigmatic people. And Doc here is, so I've been told, the most formidable of us. He's the bone man. He'll help us succeed where all others have failed."

Brian thought about the bones he'd made at his last dig, the minié ball and bayonet splintered skeletons of Confederate prisoners of war he'd unearthed near the mouth of the Potomac. He thought of Mary. She hated the idea of his coming here. He'd unearthed enough. He missed her, understood her, felt his wife and son becoming a dream in this place.

"You need to get to know us now, don't you, Miss Cam," Barnes said. "Our nuances and subtleties. It's the program now. It's in the national interest."

"One way or another, it always has been," Cam said. "Trying to know you."

"During the war," Wilkes said to Brian, "she carried copies of Jack London and Hemingway in her knapsack."

Barnes raised his glass to Cam. "Picture it: our enigmatic and ironic Miss Cam, laying there nights on the Hồ Chí Minh Trail, trying to figure out what in the world happened, wondering why in the hell those guys with the sled dogs she'd read about were now dropping all this fire-power on her head. Wondering where in the hell was Roberto Jordan?"

"During the war," Wilkes insisted, frowning at Barnes, "they had guys who came around, lectured units on American literature. To get to know us. I find that remarkable."

"You find that remarkable, do you, young captain?"

"Yes, I do. I don't care what you say. Do you think we ever had that certainty about our cause—that we would allow ourselves to see the people we were supposed to kill that clearly?"

"What do you mean 'we,' kemosabe," Barnes asked.

Brian saw Wilkes glance quickly at Cam, as if to register the effect of his words, the sensitivity he was displaying in contrast to Barnes' coarseness. It was the kind of sexual maneuvering you'd see on any dig; it made Brian feel at home.

"And what about you, Dr. Schulman?" Cam said, ignoring Wilkes. "Do you find us remarkable also? What brings you here, to make your bones?"

"You must already know my credentials."

"Yes. And I've read about your Civil War. It was something else I read, along with Jack London and Hemingway. To know you," she said, nodding to Wilkes. "There were six hundred thousand Americans killed in that war, weren't there? A respectable number."

"That's an odd way to put it."

"Did you know we have three hundred thousand missing? And four million dead. There are many bones to be made here, Dr. Schulman. But only the bones of white men, yes, Mr. Barnes?"

"White or black, brown or yellow, long as they're Americans. We is non-discriminatory, Comrade Cam."

"Of course. And during the war, Dr. Schulman," she looked at him, and he stared at her, really for the first time. She must have been in her forties, he thought, but you really couldn't see it until you were close; her face, shifting in the light, was ageless, her eyes bright and assessing, her lips full, her skin etched with fine lines around her eyes and mouth; she was beautiful, he thought, with her history. "During the war, Dr. Schulman, did you make any bones then?"

"What did you do in the war, daddy?" Barnes snorted. "The obligatory question. Hang on, boyo, before we get into all that. Before we dig up those particular bones, there's something I want you to try. Ah, here."

More Americans and Vietnamese had come into the room, filed over to the table. Barnes introduced Brian. Brian shook hands, the names flying past him, Vietnamese and English merging, in his jet lag, his sleeplessness, his sense of unreality at sitting in the enemy capital. The Americans were young, crew-cut, dressed in PX civvies, all of them soldiers assigned to the Remains Team; American soldiers, a generation later, back in Vietnam to find what was left behind of and by his generation. The Vietnamese were older; they in fact were his generation. He looked at them. The obligatory question in his own mind, trying to picture their faces as if circled by rifle sights.

"You bring it, Dương?" Barnes asked.

"Of course." Dương was wiry, his forearms corded and scarred. Hardcore, Brian thought. He had a thin, tough face and stained, chipped teeth. He was smoking. All the Vietnamese were smoking. "Yes, of course." He put a large ceramic bottle on the table. The waiter came immediately and placed a glass in front of each person. Brian suspected an initiatory ceremony.

"Nguyễn Đức Dương." Barnes introduced him again. "And what he has there is lizard wine. Wine of the lizard that bit you. To bid you welcome back." He winked at Brian.

"Lizard wine?"

"Scales of the dragon that bit you. And we wonder why they won the war. Better you can't see it, Doc." He tapped the bottle. "Think mescal. Think of the worm. And be thankful this isn't glass."

"It's disgusting," Cam said. "I never drink it. I know no Vietnamese who does. I think foreigners like it because they like to see us as primitive."

But when Barnes picked the bottle up she didn't refuse as he poured it into her glass, and then Brian's, Dương's, the others.

"To your bones, Doc," Barnes said, and drank. Brian raised the glass and drank also. It wasn't bad; sake-like. Perhaps stronger than sake. He felt its warmth spread through him with surprising speed. Into his bones.

The others at the table echoed the toast.

Cam held her glass up; she hadn't taken a drink. She locked eyes with him and then slowly brought the glass to her lips. He watched her throat moving as she swallowed. Everything was suddenly clearer. Something pulsed at his temples, in his groin. Vietnam, he thought again, as if he had to pin down the reality of being here. The waiter was putting down little dishes of sliced cucumber and *nước mắm*, fish sauce. Cam smiled slightly.

"You drink like a soldier."

"We're all soldiers here, Miss Cam," Barnes said.

"I asked what you did during the war, Dr. Schulman."

"Brian."

"Then you must call me Cam."

He shrugged. "I was aircrew during the war, Cam. Helicopters. Though I spent some time on the ground also. Mostly in Quảng Nam, Thừa Thiên-Huế, and Quảng Trị provinces."

Dương looked at him. "I was in those provinces also," he said. "I was a mortar soldier."

We're all soldiers here. Here two days before Christmas. A ditty sung in Quảng Nam or Thừa Thiên-Huế or Quảng Trị province some twenty-five Christmas eves before went through Brian's head. *Jingle Bells/Mortar shells/VC in the grass/You can take your Christmas truce/And shove it up your ass.* Who am I drinking with, here in Hanoi, he thought. "Then we have something in common."

"Were you a mortar soldier also?" Dương asked.

"No, but I was mortared."

Dương laughed. Brian clicked glasses with him. "I'm happy, sir, that you had such bad aim."

"And I am happy also, sir, that you were too blind to see me. From your noisy helicopter."

"What does it mean," Cam asked, "to be aircrew?" She wasn't smiling. "What did you do?"

"We observed," he said. And sometimes, he thought, we brought things down. On that which we observed. On those whom we observed. Sometimes we made our bones. She stared at him, their eyes locked across the table. "I hated your airplanes," she said. "The B-52s. But all of them. The bombers. The fighters. The helicopters. They killed everything. Everything on the ground. And sometimes they came down to us. The helicopters. I hated that the most."

Her eyes were hard, unforgiving.

"I hated that too, when they came down," he said, trying to lighten it. But she didn't smile. A phrase containing identical words but with a completely different meaning to each of them, he thought. A truth that seemed somehow to encapsulate this evening. She continued to stare at him, and suddenly, fiercely, he was glad, glad for her implacability, her refusal to forgive him. He took another drink of the lizard wine.

"Do you remember," Barnes said, "how we used to bullshit during the war, how one day we'd all sit around and blow weed with the VC? It was just one of those things you'd say, right?" He refilled Brian's glass.

"I would try to imagine," Cam said, "your faces. You aircrew. But you were just noise. Noise above us and the leaves and the trees shivering. Noise and terror. I tried. But I couldn't make myself believe that anything in those machines had human faces."

Brian drank deeply, looking at her face. The warmth had become heat now, pushing through his veins, just under his skin. He looked at the kids at the other end of the table, young American faces, flesh growing as he watched over the bones he was here to find; he'd seen enough of them, too, in his aircraft, on the ground. Their human faces, rotting into the ground now. Here and there. Something hardened inside him. "What did you do," he demanded of her, "in the war?"

She shook her head.

"She was in the Youth Volunteers," Dương said. "Do you know what they were?"

"They were these kids," Barnes said. He waved at the table, the young American soldiers, silent, looking at them. "Some of them high school kids from Hanoi, fifteen, sixteen years old. They used them on the Hồ Chí Minh Trail, to repair the bomb damage, defuse unexploded bombs. Sappers. But a lot of them were just these kids, these teenage girls like Cam."

He tried to picture it, picture her. "How?"

"I don't understand you."

"How did you do it? Repair the bomb damage."

"It was where I learned to dig. A skill that has become useful now, yes? If your bombs did not exploded, we tried to make them without harm. Harmless, yes? If we couldn't, we'd dig holes around them, until we could make them, how do you say? Vertical. Then they would be explode. And those holes, the . . . craters, we'd fill in. So the road could be used."

"How," he asked again, the insistent question he would ask on a dig.

"How? With shovels. Or our hands. Many of us died, doing that. You would come often, while we did that. Your airplanes. Your aircrews."

He felt the ghost of his past in this country stir in the air, saw an army of women, of teenage girls, moving under the tree canopies into which he had fired, smoothing the earth, erasing the war as they went. "Sometimes we flew over the Trail, shot down blind at it," Brian said to her, nodding, drinking it in like the wine: her hatred, her condemnation. "It was all triple canopy around there and we could never see you." He looked at her face across the table. She was staring at him also. She looked away.

"These vets," Barnes said, "come back here now, go down to the places they fought? Looking for some geographic closure or something. How about you, Doc? You one of those? You ever feel a need for a little geographic closure. On a personal level?"

Brian thought of a friend, Alex Hallam, also an ex-gunner, who'd adopted a Vietnamese girl, taking her into his home as if he had wanted to pull her out from under that mist-draped jungle canopy and into the hatch of his helicopter. "I'm an archaeologist and a forensic anthropologist; I don't really believe in closure. Whatever's been covered can always be uncovered, or sometimes even uncovers itself, works its way out of the earth. Whether you want it to or not."

"Sure as hell would make our lives easier," Barnes said. "Little thingies working their own way out."

"Hey, you know?" one of the young soldiers said, his voice drunk, his face the resentful face of a dead GI Brian had carried in his helicopter. "Fuck all you old guys. Making us spend our Christmas at your damn war."

"Yes. Fuck all us old guys." Dương nodded vigorously, looking at Cam.

"Yes," Cam said. "We must look to the future. To a future of prosperity for all. Hooray for the future. We must bury the past. The past is just a rotten nail in our heads. We must bury the past by digging up the past, yes, Dr. Schulman? We must dig up the last of you, Doctor Archaeologist-Aircrew, and send you home."

"Listen," Barnes said. "It's time to play the game. FNG's the captain, right?"

Brian had played it before, on other digs, with other archaeologists, with soldiers. Now he was the captain. The Fucking New Guy. Glasses were filled to the brim, each in turn drained; if someone didn't do it, Brian had to drink the re-filled glass. Cam drank one glass, then refused another. She watched him with what seemed to be amusement; she needed, he thought, to keep control of herself but didn't mind watching others lose it. "Good for the male strength," Dương tapped the bottle as he filled Brian's glass, and Brian felt the heat, a lizard stir in his groin. Cam sneered at him. He felt a flush of shame, then emptiness, a twist of grief, the lizard moving up, gnawing at his entrails. "I insist, I insist," Dương said, grinning at him, his face swelling and distending. "Come on, Doc, drink," he heard Barnes command, as if from a distance, and he felt the heat from the wine swirl in his throat, his head, his veins.

Barnes had filled Dương's glass again. Everybody was staring at him. Dương looked at the wine, and then at Brian. What seemed to be small silver scales speckled the liquid. The table was suddenly quiet. Brian saw Cam looking at Dương with concern. Dương's eyes swimming with distress. "Please," he said to Brian.

"No way," Brian said. "I'm your captain. It's an order. I insist."

Dương's face twitched. He tapped the glass, and then his forehead. His fingernails were broken and nicotine stained. "Quảng Trị," he said to Brian, naming, Brian understood, what the wine was opening in his head, the hot, rubber blackness of a night in Quảng Trị, split by flares and tracers, riven with screams, and Brian nodded and reached over and took Dương's glass and drained it, took it away from Dương and into himself.

He was still drunk when they brought him to the hotel, a narrow, six story Graham Greene affair of sooty concrete and iron balconies, a circle with Chinese ideograms formed into the iron gate in front of the building. The room had a narrow bed, a desk and a heavy, teak armoire. He lay on the bed and stared at the high ceiling, listening to the Vietnamese voices drifting into the grated window. A dog barked. The ceiling spun around the requisite ceiling fan. The voices merged into a dream; he was trying to teach a class of archaeology students how to read Vietnamese, writing words whose meaning he didn't know on the blackboard and pretending to the class he knew what they meant, making it up as he went along. He heard a bang in the dream and then he was awake, looking at the door. He was sure he'd heard it open. Or close. He saw a shadow, briefly, in the square of frosted glass that formed the top half of his door, but when he tried to rise, he groaned and lay back down. He turned his head sideways on the pillow; it was wet with drool. There was a jar—he was sure it hadn't been there before—on the small desk. A note was propped against it. *To Dr. Sulman, Aircrew. A happy Christmas from Miss Quảng Trị. Welcome back.* He picked up the jar. It was plastic, not glass. The liquid shifted heavily in it. A little of the wine sloshed from the top, cold on his skin, its smell turning his stomach. The lizard was gutted open, its head swollen with absorbed alcohol, its split body winged out, the ragged edges of its entrails and scaled hide tattered and waving in the current awakened by Brian's lifting. Floating in the dark liquid it seemed on the very edge of liquidity and dissolution, on the verge of sea change. Yet its form, flat-eyed, hunched and predatory, remained intact and snarling, held tentatively in the scale-flecked liquid darkness into which it refused to dissolve, rigid but curled and fetal all at once, something terrible and dead and that contained in the very shape of its death the coiled threat of rebirth.

The site they were to dig was in Hạ Long Bay, northeast of Hanoi. The aircraft, an F-105 out of Thailand on one of the early bombing missions, had been hit and crashed into one of the three thousand islands in the archipelago scattered in the Bay. Even though the crash site was known to the Vietnamese, the pilot's body had never been recovered and until the new normalization agreements, pushed into existence by Clinton, McCain and Kerry, they had not allowed an American MIA team access to the crash site. Nam Hiến, the man who was to meet the team in the town of Hồng Gai, had been in charge of the antiaircraft battery that had brought the plane down. He would guide them to the site.

They drove to Hải Phòng, took a rust-bucket ferry over to Quảng Ninh and then journeyed through a landscape of jade-green rice fields and limestone karst mountains that looked like the war. They were to meet Nam Hiến and the other Vietnamese members of the team in the banquet room of the tourist hotel where the search team was booked. It was Christmas Eve. In the lobby, several young men—military age males, thought Brian—were sitting around a television, watching a music video and singing karaoke into a hand mike, a small plastic

Christmas tree set up on the table next to them. A photograph of Hồ Chí Minh and a red star decorated the wall behind the banquet table.

Nam Hiến was a stocky, dark-skinned man with bright eyes and a strong grip, something Brian noticed when they met and shook hands and later during the meal and the seemingly inevitable drinking bout after it, whenever he'd tell a story or direct Brian to a new item of food. That hard press against his skin seemed either deliberately punishing or as if he needed to test Brian's reality. "Quảng Nam, Thừa Thiên-Huế, Quảng Trị," Brian said. "Yes," Nam Hiến said. *We're all soldiers here.* They ate blood oysters and shrimp cakes embedded with whole shrimps and drank bottle after bottle of Heineken and Tiger beer. As if they had to go someplace else together, Brian thought. As if they had to become new stories to each other.

"I'll tell you a story," Nam Hiến said, Cam translating for Brian. His unit had been the first here to shoot down an American plane. Their antiaircraft gun had been located next to the building where they sat now. "Not this building though," Cam interjected. "Most of this place was destroyed by your bombings." No, right here, Hiến insisted, gripping Brian's arm hard. "An A-7, was that right?" The pilot had ejected, fallen into the Bay. They had jumped into a boat and raced out to him. Raced against all the fishing boats and sampans trying to get to him first. They, the soldiers, were afraid the fishermen would kill the pilot. And the fishermen got to him first. The fishermen grabbed the white silk top of the chute floating in the water and pulled the pilot up: they began beating him with sticks and poles with metal fingers on their ends—gaff hooks, Brian supposed Cam meant. Began pushing him back under, she translated. Hiến and his soldiers yelled at them, and then Hiến went over the side. He grabbed the pilot as he was going deeper under, pulled him up to the air. The front of the man's flying suit—flight suit, Brian translated in his mind—was ripped open and Hiến remembered being startled, seeing nothing but wet, black, body fur. Thinking, in that instant, *you see, it is true, they are not us, they are beasts.* The American was still sinking, and when Hiến gripped him, Cam said, he screamed. Hiến could see it under the water, the scream becoming a silver bubble escaping from the pilot's mouth. But he held on, gripped the pilot's arm tightly and drew him back to the surface, he said, clutching Brian's arm, his fingers pushing in painfully on Brian's bicep.

They drank. Then they went out into town, Brian and the Vietnamese: the other Americans stayed back in the hotel. The street was mobbed. Groups of people—families or friends—clustered together within the crowd, which was pushing out along the paths winding up the steep slope of the mountain to which the town clung. Laughing, singing, eating, drinking, lighting sparklers and shooting off firecrackers. Climbing to what Cam said was a bombed-out cathedral on the crest. It was the way Hồng Gai celebrated Christmas. A town without Christians, he thought. There were many Catholics in the North, Cam explained. "But many also who are not Catholic," she said. "Who were just Vietnamese people in a town which was bombed." Now Vietnamese people pressed in on all sides of him, their skins hot and damp from the exertion of the climb, the celebration. They stared at him. Most of them were too young to have been here during the war, he told himself. Hello, hello, children called to him. The crowd pressed in. A string of fireworks went off in long staccato bursts, the sharp stench of cordite mixing with the smell of charcoal and cooking meat and sweat. A film, shot-down flyers paraded before a screaming mob, faces distorted with hate, began to roll through his mind. He thought about how Dương had tapped his head, naming what was being set loose in it by the lizard wine. He had no name for what was being unmoored in him now, tight wound cables snapping in his head. He stopped, looked around wildly. Someone clutched his right hand. Someone else clutched the other. Dương had come up on his right side, Hiến on the other, and they gripped his hands tightly, the crowd looking at the two veterans and making a space for them that he moved in as they pulled him up the path to the top of the mountain. He could see the city, a broken outline of lights, a jumble of concrete blocks built since the war, lying below them, spread down the slope and on the apron of land against the Bay. Looking up, he could see the cathedral at the crest, the point of convergence for the crowd, a jagged shell, roofless, a reminder of the war, of the peace that had not yet been built. There was an altar at the east wall, people lighting candles and incense in front of it. Hiến and Dương held onto his hands tightly and he gripped theirs, the two of them pulling him out of the dark water into which he had been falling.

They took Christmas Day off. Brian slept through most of it, though on the boat the next morning he still felt queasy and his head throbbed. Hiến, standing in the bow, smiled and waved at him, and Dương brought him a cup of bitter green tea. Cam looked away, her face expressionless.

The day was misty. The boat glided through a maze of karst islands, jagged and worn and mossy as bad teeth. He tried to imagine how it would have been, to fly from some carrier or base in Guam or Thailand into the dragon fangs of this weird landscape.

"There," Hiến called.

The boat had emerged from a channel and was coming around the side of an island, its cliff rising hundreds of feet above them. Just above the indented ring of white rock that circled the base of the karst, marking the tide level, were the two black entrances of a cave system. High above the cave was a flat shelf, like a single gigantic step cut into the cliff face, a copse of trees bristling on it. Brian looked back down. A small sampan glided past them, a child and a dog sitting in front of the palm frond thatched shelter on its bow, behind them a woman cooking on a charcoal brazier, and a cone-hatted fisherman standing at the stern tiller, all of them ignoring him, into their own lives. A red flag fluttered from the top of the little shelter, its green fronds somehow echoing the trees clustered on the karst. He looked again at the cliff, the two eyes of the cave, and saw a path etched to its right, up to the small plateau, and another visual echo there, another small red flag marking the site where they would dig.

It took them two hours to get to the top and another hour to set up the sifting trays and other equipment. The Vietnamese had roped off the site already. The starred mark of the impact where the plane had hit was overgrown, but some of that foliage had been hacked away. At least it was soil there, rocky, but not solid rock as he first had feared. The digging would be difficult but not impossible. He wondered how much of the area had been caused by the crash itself, if any. But if there had been any surface debris from the plane—there had to be, he thought—it had been cleared long before. He staked out lines for two trenches bisecting the most likely area of impact, and then gridded the area with stakes and string.

The younger Americans and the Vietnamese formed a bucket line, bringing soil and rocks to the sifting trays. He and Hiến stood side by side, watching the dirt as it fell through the wire grid of the tray, looking for any objects: bits of metal or singed cloth or canvas or, better, anything with a name or part of a name on it, or, best of all, bone. A piece or pieces of Lieutenant Commander Anthony Deramus of Gambier, Ohio, survived by a wife, now remarried, and two children, both as old now as the kids working for him on this team. Lieutenant Commander Deramus, missing yet perhaps on the cusp of being found. But nothing sifted through the soil, sand, and rock, which left behind itself only a ghost of white dust that caked their skin.

"Hey, Doc," Barnes called. "I think we got something."

Brian walked over to the other side of the trench.

"Here," Barnes said, patting.

Brian patted the same area, gently. He could feel the cylindrical shape, just under the skin of the earth, perfect, too perfect. Is this you, Mr. Deramus? "Good call," he said to Barnes. Dương came over and then Cam, both squatting down near him. He brushed the earth aside with his bristle, gently, layer by dermic layer, and he could see it now, brown and aged. But too wide. Like the finger bone of a giant.

He started to move down it, further and further, using his spade now to evacuate a little surrounding trench, but it went on and on, too far, until Dương's hand came down and stopped his, and Dương reached down further into the trench and pulled it all up, a pointed wooden stake, black and brown and soft rotted in places.

"*Hang Đầu Gỗ*," he said. Brian looked at Cam, who had gotten up and was standing next to him, hitting her hands against her thighs.

"'The Cave of the Sharpened Stakes,'" she translated. "It's on another island, near this one. Trần Hưng Đạo, the emperor. When the Mongols invaded us, he hid many thousands of such stakes on these islands. Most to be put underwater, to, how do you say, rip the bottom of ships. Or smaller, on land, to rip the bottom of horses' legs. Or men. The Mongols came in a large force. Three hundred thousand."

"A respectable number," Brian said.

She ignored him. "Destroying everything," she said. "We let them come deep into us. Then we destroyed them."

She turned her face away.

"When was that?" Brian asked, looking at the stake, trying to date it. He wondered if the Vietnamese smeared them with shit then also. When they set them into the earth rather than the rivers. When they used them against the Mongols.

"Thirteenth century," Dương said. He started to laugh. He explained the find rapidly, in Vietnamese, and then the others joined in and the Americans also, all of them looking at each other caked with soil, enjoying the sudden release of tension. But Cam, Brian saw, didn't join them. She had squatted again at the lip of the trench, staring at the weapon that had refused to soften into the earth around it or remain buried, her face clenched with grief or disappointment.

Hiến, at one of the sifting trays, called out to Brian. He held up what he had found: a small piece of metal. Brian took it, caressing the smoothness, the sharp edges. It was black, nameless and numberless, but it was their first piece of the plane, another weapon buried in this soil. He grinned at Hiến and nodded. Hiến smiled back and spoke rapidly. He looked around and saw Cam working in the ditch near him as if nothing had happened, her hands, brown, blunt-fingered, capable, carefully parting the earth as she once had as a teenage girl, trying not to awaken a bomb. She looked up at him. "Would you mind translating," he asked.

"He said he was very excited," she said.

"I can see that."

Hiến spoke again. He was no longer smiling.

"No," Cam said. "He is excited about what we have found now also, but he means then. What we found—it makes him think of the day they shot the plane down." Hiến nodded, spoke more. "He says, they had been bombed a few times by then, but that time was the first he had caught the airplane in, how is it? The circle which you put your eye on to aim?"

"His sight," Brian said.

She shook her head. "No. Where his sight went, the aiming circle. The airplane dropped its bombs on the town and there was a great noise as houses collapsed. But inside that, he says, he was inside a silence and felt, how do you say? Glued? No. As if there was a very straight line drawn from inside him, through his eyes and hands to the gun, the plane. He says that he knew then that he would hit the plane. And when he did, it twisted up, very slowly, and then came down, very quickly. He saw that."

Hiến smiled, said something else softly.

She frowned. "He says, he saw that future clearly. That instant when he would hit the plane. But that was war, he says. But he never saw this future: that one day he would stand here with an American friend, digging to build a peace."

"Do you share his feelings?"

"I think they are exaggerated. For your benefit."

"Why bother?"

"Oh, everybody wants to turn from the war now, turn to the future. To you. Your money. Your power. To be only for themselves."

"You sound like you miss the war."

She met his stare, smiled slightly.

"No," she said. "It was terrible. It was terrible and wonderful. It was like always being in love." She shook her head. "No. I say that wrong. It was like always *falling* in love. That first minute. Do you understand how wonderful and terrible that is? What you have. What you can lose." She put her fingers into the dirt, pushing in. "I was always hungry. Once a mushroom forced me to take a tin of meat he had. Those were the drivers. Mushrooms," she said, to the question on his face. "Because of the helmets they wore. In the bombing they would just keep driving, even if they were being blown up. Because of love. And I fell in love with that driver. It's as I say. I fell in love every day. That was near Khe Sanh. In Quảng Trị, where you were above me. The bombing was so bad, we hadn't had food for a long time. We girls. We were eating roots. But sharing whatever we had. And we had stopped bleeding, we shared that too; we thought we were no longer women. From your poison. That driver had to force me to take that tin because what we had, we saved for the fighters and drivers like him, and I was ashamed. But I took it and my friends and I sat and we ate it very quickly. My stomach holding around each small piece like I had a fist inside me. I was so busy eating I did not pay attention when your planes came. When your bombs fell. I remember hearing a great noise outside but also inside my head. And later I woke up and all the trees were gone and all the trucks and the mushrooms and my friends were gone and I was alone in the middle of a hole, no a *crater*, and everywhere I could see were *craters* and everything was silent and my country was gone. I thought this is how a ghost sees the world."

She turned from him, her eyes brimming, but her mouth set and tough.

Get some, they would say, and cheer when they'd hear and see the bombings, Brian remembered, and looking at her he saw it, saw her waking, a young woman utterly alone under the suddenly silent sky where sometimes he would hang.

She squatted next to the trench. Her shoulders, he saw, were trembling. He squatted down next to her, understanding suddenly how she would see this work he had felt compelled to take up, the wound he would rip into a wound, and then, a part of him thinking she would find it sentimental and romantic or presumptuous, a part of him not thinking very much at all, he began clawing at the pile of dirt and rock, pulling it back into the trench. "What are you doing?" Dương called out to him, laughing, and then Hiến and the others called out also, Barnes staring at him, but he ignored them. Cam smiled sardonically at him and shrugged, dismissing, he understood, his costless and tardy gesture. But, for an instant anyway, a moment suspended in time, she began to help him, scooping in the rocks and dirt, filling in what he had opened in the ground, her hands smoothing the earth as if erasing words only she could see written upon it.

MEDEVAC

STANDING BY FOR MISSIONS, HE ALWAYS HAS THE FEEL-
ing he is being centered in the lens of a movie camera. Flight suit and
sunglasses, focused in sharply by the magnifying clearness of the
Danang air. A loud buzzer sounds with dramatic insistence. A long
shot: the crews running self-consciously to the helicopters, loading
machine guns competently, talking flight talk, sticking their thumbs
up. Switch to the interior of the helicopter; the lens zooms in for a really
fine shot of his sweaty, grease-stained face framed over his machine
gun by the open port. Then a full shot of the interior: the black crew
chief pumping the A.P.E, then running forward to his gun, black and
white at the opposite ports, the subtle impact of the scene: no racists
in foxholes, by God.

The sun sinks as the helicopter rises. The gunner looks at its fall and
feels powerful and full of height. In its wake, the sun begins sucking
the colors out of the ground, and the earth seems insignificant to him.

The crew talks on the intercom, the cords on their helmets and their
voices linking them in the darkness. They are flying towards Dong Ha.
Hastily to Hastings, the gunner thinks. Operation Hastings. Where did
they get the names? He is trying to slide his sight through the darkness,
looking for flashes, for tracers, for anything. For today's trick we will

clear the DMZ with Norman cavalrymen. They must be catching shit, he thinks, to be calling for planes on secondary alert. Means the choppers already at Dong Ha are very full, and the crews will be cleaning out the insides with hoses, washing away any spare bleeding parts left sticking on the helicopters' decks.

The trap door of a gallows suddenly opens, right at the moment when he is counting on more time. A drop and a wait for the noose to snap his neck.

The helicopter falls, then seems to catch itself, and circle down more lazily. Leaning out of his port, he can see the flashes of the strobe the grunts are using to mark the landing zone, but the light doesn't illuminate the terrain. The aircraft drops into darkness. The noose never tightens.

The helicopter lands hard and the rear ramp drops heavily. The gunner stays at his gun while the crew chief runs back to help with the wounded. Looking over the barrel, he can just make out part of the circle of infantrymen around the Zone. Their green backs look tense and they are mud-spattered and somehow fragile-looking in their hardness. They don't look as if they'd stepped off a tapestry. Backs and saggy asses and legs and boots. Too normal for Normans.

The wounded come through the open rear hatch, touching the sides of the helicopter with gentle, bloody hands. They are already a race apart, consecrated in the eyes of the unwounded, receivers of blows meant for the unhurt. Some intact Marines are carrying in those unable to walk and laying them out on the deck. The helicopter is filling up and its blades beat the air insistently as if feeling the danger and straining to go. The wounded are twisted into one another, holding onto each other, softly bleeding into each other's wounds. The gunner strains for comparisons, sees a pile of soiled laundry, cloth arms and legs locked into impossible positions. Or pudding. Bleeding pudding. Hastings pudding.

The ramp closes and the helicopter lifts. A corpsman moves among the Marines, shooting morphine into them. Many haven't been treated at all yet. We must have landed right in the middle of something, the gunner thinks.

A Marine, his torn trousers showing shredded meat, is trying to stand up next to the gunner, leaving more room for the worse wounded. He puts his hand on the gunner's shoulder to steady himself, then looks at him apologetically. The gunner turns away for a second and notices the black man lying near his feet. The man seems to have a red gelatinous mass growing from the side of his neck, twisting his head and strangling him. His eyes bulge.

All this in a second, a split second, for he is dutifully looking out of the port and doesn't miss the flashes below and the green tracers flying up at the helicopter. He fires his guilt down at the flashes and feels it leave him in violent spurts through the machine gun barrel. Just shooting at our noise, he thinks; they're too far. His own tracers flash red. Maybe I hit some NVA, he thinks, and he's being dragged off on a hook by his buddy. Who's feeling guilty the hook ain't in his own pudding neck. Fucking fool. The firing stops.

Then they are dropping towards Dong Ha, and are down, and the ramp drops again.

The corpsmen come in with some service troops who have volunteered to carry stretchers. See what they've been missing. The bearers are in respectful awe of the wounded, but try to act as nonchalant as the corpsmen. The walking wounded begin walking and the gunner helps the man who had been leaning next to him walk out, then turns back inside.

The corpsmen are going through the men lying on the deck, quickly, competently, placing two enchanted fingers on wrists, bestowing life or death. The stretcher-bearers begin lifting one man; the corpsman is still touching his wrist. Save it, the corpsman advises, he's bought it. The dead man is a big blond boy.

"Save it," the economical corpsman says, and gestures impatiently at the volunteers. "Get'm out quick; he can't feel nothin'." One of the bearers grabs the man's ankles and drags the body out. The head bounces up and down on the ramp, as the body slides, then thuds dully on the ground.

Save what? The gunner thinks.

He goes out and walks away from the fuel lines and tries to catch a quick smoke before they take off again.

THE LAST VC

"AND WHAT EXOTIC ISLE D'YE HAIL FROM?" THE UNION soldier asks me.

"Florida, muthafucka," I answer. The other girls crack up. The Union soldier has his act, I have mine. He's Black and wears blue. I wear black. Other people dressed in history clothes parade back and forth on the grass. Me there to see the Ghost Tour with the other girls from Ruth's House, daffies, Disturbed Adolescent Females, the counselors think we don't know that label. Last week we went to Historic Maryland, saw the Founders' Ship, you can go on board but nothing happens on it like Pirates of the Caribbean or anything, you just look at the sailors' hammocks and some barrels and go uh-huh. There wasn't much else. Just a visitor center look like a barn 'cause it was a barn and an inn (dumb daffies singing we in the inn) and a brick building suppose to be the first capital, only the people looked around and said oh shit, the boonies, and left. That's it. Except for some little roped-off places with signs telling you to believe that buried under the dirt is a tavern or plantation or slave house or whatever they want to say is there. One little sign says trash midden: this window set into the ground like the glass-bottom boat, what you see through it is four hundred years of dirty oyster shells and smashed up plates and cups and chewed on bones. This garbage under everything.

"A saucy wench," the soldier says, winking at me. I give him my hooded, cool look, VCWA, Viet Cong With An Attitude, then look

27

away, staring around the area. Near the beach this big cannon, around it, on the lawn, these white pyramid tents, campfires, a fence made from long sharp top logs, everything blinking into existence as I look like the Star Trek holodeck where you can have any scene you want. For a minute I play with the scene being different for each group or individual that comes in, fitting these holes in their minds. If I did a theme park, that's what it would be.

"K-K no saw-see 'xotic eye," Tonetta says to the Union, putting her hands on both sides of her face and pulling up the skin above her eyes to show him what I am. "K-K jus' a gook."

The other girls giggle, say gook, gook, like a flock of daffies, these disturbed dyslexi-assed ducks who'd fuck up their quack. Tonetta must have picked the gook up from the tape we saw last night, *Platoon*. Tonetta pushing me to start Physical Confrontation, so I'll lose my privilege level. I'm cool though, smile at her, while I flip Mario mushrooms out of the top of my head. They arc through the air, smack Tonetta, she puffs to nothing with a blip. On I float, to the next obstacle. Which is, Tonetta smiles back at me, rubs and pats her rounded tummy with lovely tenderness. Bam. King Koopa zaps Mario, all five lives blink out. Tonetta came into the program too late for an abortion and now she rubs her big black ripe melon belly in my face every chance she gets, whenever she can't get at me with words or hands. Every chance, all the time, knowing the counselors were giving me BC pills, standing over me and watching me swallow, knowing if they didn't I would swell, put another mutant out in the world. Why? For company, muthafucka. That's why.

"Ladies," Louise, the counselor, says. "Behave. No verbal abuse."

"K-K started it," Tonetta says.

"That's Kiệt, please," Louise says.

"Shee-it, whatever," Tonetta says, and the other girls laugh. I am pissed at Louise for bringing it up. My name. I was Keisha when I came to Ruth's House from Crownsville Detention, but Larry got hold of my exotic I-land papers and he found Kiệt, drew that name out of the muck at the bottom of the sea, little hat supposed to draw over the e, little turd dot under it, this old bone memory he wanted me to wrap around with my new skin. I had to explain to him that name was all drowned, all shriveled up and fish nibbling its eye sockets, so I tried being reasonable and said go with K-K, but he tells me no, you need to be proud of your heritage. Meaning the gook part I didn't know fuck-all about, this from Larry, he's black but he's a vet, which is like this other color, something between black and puke green. Even though later I found on my own Kiệt really a boy's name and Larry fucked that up. Never mind. In my head I was and still am K-K. Half-a-dink, half-a-splib my foster dad used to call me, both his way of saying nigger.

But meanwhile the banana-gana bonanna name game further pisses Tonetta off, Tonetta getting her name from the cat in her first or second or whatever foster home had tried to keep her. The way she had left that place, Tonetta the kid had hung Tonetta the cat with a lamp cord to which I can relate, but still it wasn't the cat's idea. Animals get fucked over. Like, my ex-foster father I'd run away from, in Florida? He let me go to Sea World once and I smoked some dope before I went and then watched the Flipper show. Flipper this dolphin who did all of these kissy-ass doggy-type tricks for these people in wet suits that were suppose to be its TV family, though I never saw the sitcom, it was suppose to be famous. I watched and I started to identify and cry from the reefer opening me up to things, lighting up things it touched like an old pinball game. Like what do you think that dolphin's real name was? Something like Glub-Cluck. Or Fuk Luck. Or Kiệt. Swimming around. Thinking to itself: what's this Flipper shit?

"Come on, ladies," Larry said. "We'll be late for the Historical Reenactment."

We shuffle past towards the tents, next to an open field. Prisoners in raggy gray, white guys, and guards with bayonet rifles and blue Union uniforms, most of them black—sure, fuck me—walk around like fools. Inside one tent they pretending to cut off these dummies' arms and legs, more white guys in phony looking blood-stained aprons sawing away, the daffies going gag and barf. We pass an old black mama wearing a white hood and an apron; she's sitting in front of a kind of small barrel, stirring a stick in it in hard circles. I stop to look, but really to let Larry get in front of me cause Larry's stare is on my skin like dirty spider webs, this scared kind of sideway interest in me he got, not a sex thing, but like always looking at me for something, booby traps, I don't know what.

Stir, stir, stir. Like last night, we were watching the *Platoon* tape and this scene where the bad sergeant Tom Berenger blows away this mother and threatens to kill her kid. The other daffies going burn or shoot or giggling, they're so bone ignorant, while I'm wondering if that was how someone did my real mom. On the screen all the GI's fighting with each other whether they should waste all the gooks or what and I don't know which side my real dad would have been on, raggy gray or blue, some of the splib soldiers in the movie were on Berenger's side, some on the good sergeant's side, and I was Charlie Sheen, split in half, I could feel them all inside of me. Stir, stir, stir. Willem Dafoe, he played the good sergeant.

So I got out of the room and sat on the couch in the office upstairs, in the dark. And sure enough, Larry came up after me. He went to switch on the light. Leave it off, I told him.

"Bad movie," he said, sitting down next to me, big and heavy and kind of leaning into me, not in any kind of coming on way, but like he was really trying to see me, in the dark, moonlight coming in the window, splitting my face, Keisha blocked out, only the tipped up Kiệt eyes showing, like the eyes of his enemy. Or maybe some woman he remembered, some love he left swollen with a half-a-dink half-a-splib mutant to come swimming after him one day. When I'd run away from Florida to DC, I ran to the Wall I'd seen on TV. The Wall took the high yellow out of my face and gave it back to me black, black with the white names scrawled all over it. I had walked along it slowly, letting the names write themselves across my skin, if my daddy's name was there it would have stayed on my skin when I turned from it.

"Who cares?" I said.

Larry shifted his weight, a creaking black heaviness next to me, the sounds of the movie drifting to us in the dark like a Historical Reenactment, screams and explosions and voices from this place where we first became some kind of garbage under each other's lives.

"Don't mean nothin'," he said, a saying from the war, and I remember Historic Maryland, how he and Louise had herded the daffies into a little room, a sign: Sensurround Theatre over its door. The inside walls covered with pictures like inside the old time Founders' Ship. We sat on benches. The doors shut. The lights went out. A voice started whispering, trickling into my brain like Larry's whisper. The movie played on all the walls around me. Creaking ropes. Waves. A voice said: "Hardship and starvation." I saw flickering people packed into the thin space of a wooden boat, heard their screams and moans, smelled their sour puke, shit, piss, the stink of *nước mắm* fish sauce. Sensurround. "The New World," the voice said. The lights flashed on. The movie was over.

Now a park ranger in a Smokey the Bear hat stands in front of us, megaphone in one hand, little cassette recorder in the other. Starts talking about how here on this ground under our feet blah-blah one of the largest prisoner-of-war camps from the Civil War, thirty thousand Confederate prisoners here, exposed to weather and abuse and all in Maryland. Talks about black feds being guards. Talks about payback. While he's going on, this ragged ass white prisoner runs away and the sharp black guard I saw before raises his musket, shoots him down. Right. Just like real life. Only the prisoner too raggedy to look white. Smeared and gray. A dink. Other place, three soldier guards, black and white, pretend to beat down another prisoner.

"They really get into it," I hear Louise whisper to Larry.

"And vice versa," he says.

Smokey the Bear talks about how if you leave out recorders here, at night, no one around, they pick up these ghost voices he's going to let us listen to. He turns on the recorder. Garble, garble, the voices say.

We walk back over to the tents, little fires and stacked pyramids of old-time guns propped against each other in front of each tent.

"Muskets," Louise says, explaining the New World as if to someone who gave a fuck. People are taking pictures of other people, some in the tents. A man is stuffing a little boy into the mouth of a cannon. The kid's mother is taking pictures.

"Look terrified, Jason," she says. "Stop grinning like a dork."

A group of Union soldiers march by us, led by this roostery old white man. The soldiers, black and white, are all waddley, fat bellies pushing out their uniform shirts over their belts: fat old men daffies led by a rooster. Too old to be soldiers. Or like soldiers kept forever in the army for a forever war.

Somebody beats a drum. The soldiers get into this kind of raggy line, facing me. They point their muskets at me, Run, run, run, run, run, the voices on the tape say to me. The rooster man pulls out a sword and yells readyaimfire. The flash and the noise split me in half. Blow Kiệt away from Keisha. Dink from splib.

I squint at the soldiers. They load and fire again. If I worked here I'd play a VC. I'd squat near the entrance to a reconstruct straw hootch, rocking my baby, waiting while the tourists, all dressed as GIs came into the village. Then I'd rise up, reveal the weapon hidden under my baby and pretend to blow them away. Then one day I'd forget where I really was. I'd put real bullets into the gun. I'd have a flashback and shoot a tourist, thinking he was Tom Berenger, come to rape and murder. Then, before anyone realized what happened, I'd run. I'd hide in the marshes. I'd be the last VC.

"Fire!" the rooster squawks.

The soldiers load and fire again.

"Fix bayonets," the rooster says.

The soldiers stick their bayonets on the ends of their muskets. They point them at me and charge, yelling, their faces twisted.

I back up a little bit from the faces and stumble into Tonetta. She curses me under her breath and pushes me into one of the stacks of muskets. They fall with a clatter. The soldiers stop a few feet from me and threaten with their bayonets. I pick up one of the fallen guns.

"Look terrified, bitch," I say to Tonetta.

"Kiệt, put that down," Larry says. He steps in front of me. I see myself reflected in his shades, black-clad, holding a weapon.

"We're here now," I tell him. I point the gun at him.

He looks at me and backs up, funny smile on his face.

"Don't mean nothin'," I tell him.

"For your own safety," the announcer on the PA says, "please do not handle the weapons."

The musket is heavier than I thought it would be. I wonder what will happen. Everybody is looking at me. You can't trust the gooks, I'd say. Then I'd pull the trigger. The flash would leap out and hit Larry's chest. Maybe he'd have a heart attack and die, his last sight: my face. Or maybe he'd jump at me. I'd club his hands and turn and run.

Even as I think this, I club down at his hands and then I am running, a part of me still running in my head, but my feet really pounding against the grass. I zigzag in the direction of the parking lot, holding onto the musket. Behind me I hear Louise and Larry calling K-K as if to please me, but I keep on running: what's this Flipper shit? If I look over my shoulder now, I know I'll see the two of them and the camp guards and the prisoners, all chasing me, muskets in their hands, their faces red and angry. I know I'll see armies of mad old men, all dressed like soldiers, all chasing after me.

THE
VIETNAMESE
ELECTIONS

ONCE THERE WERE DOGS IN THE SQUADRON AT MARBLE Mountain. There had always been a bunch of them wandering around the base, infiltrating in from the highway and from the huts strung like dirty straw beads along the roadside. Vietnamese dogs, skinny and hungry, but with eyes and acts like any dogs, Free World or Communist Conspiracy. They'd look at you reproachfully if you didn't feed them, piss on your tent or the colonel's, all of the things that made dogs attractive to Americans.

Some became special. Adopted.

The squadron had three dogs. One to Motor T, one to Avionics and one to Operations. Each dog had one guy who took care of him, but he belonged to all of them. Hanging around the flight line. Watching the crews coming back from missions. Getting in people's way. Getting cursed. Getting their ears scratched and their asses kicked. You know, dogs and Americans.

The dogs were three, thus:

To Avionics: A yellow almost cocker spaniel called Grease.

To Ops: Herbert, black and white and three teeth.

To Motor T: A large and strange half-boxer, half-setter called Ky. He had a habit of farting in formation.

Some permitted pats on the head from outsiders; all would take food from whomever they could get it, and all were completely chauvinistic towards their particular section. It got them a lot of kicks and started a lot of fights.

The order came:

FROM:
TO:
SUBJECT:

there are too many dogs here and I'm supposed to do something, after all I'm c.o. of the base and it's unhygienic and what are we here for anyway kill japs kill japs, you'll do your job better if you only have one dog per squadron.

The rest to be shot.

Sincerely yours,
America

So, they had to shoot two dogs.

The C.O. decided on an election. "First Shirt, we'll have a formation and do it democratically."

"Squadron, atten-HUT!"

Ky farted. So did Torenelli.

The dogs were held in their keeper's arms. They squirmed and tried to jump down onto the flight mat but were held tightly. They were having a good time.

Democracy started.

The C.O. was in the admin tent signing air medal certifications. So, the First Sergeant read the order. It was an impressive ceremony.

If you could have seen it all from the air, as Lieutenant DeLeon was doing at that very moment from his helicopter, it would have really looked inspiring. The base lying beneath him like a gridiron hand laid pressed on the land.

Look. First an ocean (the South China Sea), turquoise blue and sparkling, interspaced with patches of deep green. Next to the ocean and startling in contrast, a large stretch of gleaming white sand held between two mountain formations (one called Marble, the other Monkey). In the middle of the stretch of sand, a great settlement: rows of tents and tin huts, huge squares of latticed metal pressed against the earth. In the middle of it all, something that could have been the center of a military-industrial complex but was really the mess hall.

On the biggest square of perforated metal were rows of helicopters, green and expensive. UH-34Ds, CH-46s, UH-1Es. And smack between the parked helicopters and a row of tents, Lieutenant DeLeon could see a geometric formation of standing men, fitting in well with the scene. Neat rows of green men at attention. Clean, handsome men who had built the order around them. Three of them were holding dogs. One of the dogs kept farting.

The keepers were each supposed to make a little speech about his dog. So, one by one, they stood with their animal in front of the staring formation, to let them decide.

"Well," they said, embarrassed, "he's a good dog."

"He's a good dog."

"He's a good dog."

The dogs looked at the men and struggled to be free, barking joyously, wanting to run and play around the forest of stiff green legs. Then someone said they should take the dogs away while the voting happened.

Okay.

Ky won. Even if some didn't vote.

They took the other two dogs behind the flight-line tents and put bullets into their brains. Later they were driven out to the trash dump and burned.

THAT MINUTE

IT WAS AS IF THEY HAD STEPPED OUT TO A DIFFERENT planet where everything was familiar but somehow off. Like aliens had seen movies or sucked memories out of people's brains, and then had turned away and built from their impressions. As if they had *paraphrased* a town. Ridge wasn't sure why he saw everything that way. It was Sunday. A sunny Sunday. In front of him a wide, tree-lined, main street picketed with parking meters, a traffic light swaying overhead. A drug store (Rexall), a movie theatre (*The Ten Commandments*), a family restaurant (Randy's). People inside perched on stools at the zinc counter or sitting in vinyl-cushioned booths. Like exhibits of themselves. To his eyes. The women in pastel Sunday dresses, beehive hairdos and make-up that froze their faces into lacquered masks; the men in white shirts and black jackets or in checkered shirts, jeans or overalls, long, narrow faces held between the parentheses of sideburns.

Ridge clicked his vision outside the restaurant again, looking at the scene in increments, per training. The phrase: *If You Like Home Cooking, Stay the "H" Home* etched on the big street-side window of Randy's. Three steepled churches: two Baptist, one Methodist. A sign in front: *God is Watching*. Three old men on a bench, staring like God's spies at him and his friends. The traffic light hanging over the intersection turned green. A rust-red Ford, its rear window painted in swirls of dust, moved forward. A Chevy pickup, happy Lab setter in the back, pink tongue flecking foam into the breeze. Down the street what might be a town hall, red brick; he imagined a little square in front, pecan trees dapple-shading the statue of a Confederate General. A *prototype* of a Southern town, Ridge thought; would that be the word? His friend Robby, who must be from a town just like this in South Carolina, thought of Ridge as a New York intellectual because he had some books in his footlocker. *A Stone for Danny Fisher, Lord of the Rings, The Agony and the Ecstasy. Webster's New World Dictionary.* Seeing the latter, Robby, six foot three, two hundred and fifty pounds, a GED dropout like Ridge, had insisted on a program to improve his vocabulary, help him *possess*, he said, his new experiences. It was something the other three in the fire team had gotten into, styling themselves educated warriors, memorizing two new words—chosen by Ridge— each day. *Misogynist. Anachronism.* Ridge's own store of words accumulating as a result.

Displacement. Alienation.

But no, he admitted, this was no strange planet. He was just in America. As opposed to being in Marine Corps. Though he could see tendrils of the Corps now, insinuated among the other buildings. A bar, (Gunny's Slop Chute), another, (Rosie's), two pawn shops. But subtract those and his imagined Confederate General and this could be his own hometown. The strangeness in his eyes, he understood, obtained from the disorganized, discombobulated *civilianness* of it all. Was that a word, Robby? The town existed because of the base it clung to like a lamprey. But it was on Earth. He and the other three with him now were the ones from a different planet, aliens from the Planet of the Marines. Camp Geiger Tigers. Infantry Training Regiment. From which they would graduate to another planet. The Planet of Vietnam. His own vision had shifted. He saw things *symmetrically.* What was unsymmetrical put him off. People diddybopping down the street out of step, maintaining erratically different intervals, hair of many lengths, clothes of many colors, shoes of many scuffs, arms flying and flailing every which way, worse, hands thrust into pockets, fingers fingering and scratching, mouths gaping, yawning, smiling, smoking, joking, slumping, chewing, spitting. Dissimilar or dysfunctional physiques. Overalls falling straight down, waist to heels, pouched over an absence of ass or straining in front to hold in a bowling ball of a belly, a woman swinging hips wide as a dumpster, hair piled multi-layered and multicolored atop her head like an ice cream sundae. It had all become strange to his eyes. He was a *spectator*, outside the bubble, he and Robby and Chris and Anton in their spotless Class A uniforms, three knife-sharp creases on the backs of their shirts, two in the front, rifle badges centered exactly over their chest pockets, shoes spit-shined so fine that tiny suns flared from their tips, piss-cutter caps square on their heads, whitewall (or in Anton's case, he supposed, blackwall) haircuts. They were a single crea-ture, fine-tuned, in-step, flat-bellied, wind-burned, taut-muscled. They finished each other's sentences or didn't have to, shared a vocabulary that wasn't in Webster's and a set of references that they had earned and now owned. Twelve weeks at Parris Island, D.I.'s spittle still on their faces, fist bruises still on their bellies, curses still ringing in their ears; four weeks at Lejeune, working together as a fire team, running four miles a day, twenty mile hikes, sixty-pound packs; field-stripping and cleaning and firing M-14 rifles and M-60 machine guns and M-1's and Browning Automatic Rifles left over from Korea at cardboard VC, throwing grenades, sneaking and peeping through thick woods and mucked swamps on nighttime compass navigations, sleeping in holes, jumping the space between two second story windows in full gear, climbing ropes in same, crawling under barbed wire, rounds cracking overhead, shot at and missed, shit at and hit. The four of them walking down this chaotic, disorganized street now, automatically in step, arms swinging six inches to the front, three to the rear, ChrisAntonRidgeRobby: Jersey boy, Marylander, New Yorker and redneck, all knit into the same body, a life-form from another planet. They had each other's backs. No matter they were beaming to Planet Vietnam. They would die for each other. Brothers. Guardians of these soft, sloppy *mundane* civilians.

The word civilians in his head somehow brought up, *conjured*, of all things, the image of an English muffin. Himself back in White Plains, when he'd worked at the A&P all through junior and senior high before and after he'd dropped out, herding shopping carts from the parking lot. He and Nick Bachman paid to rove the area, search out the carts people would roll away into the parking lots and garages and alleys and hallways of the apartment buildings around the A&P and bring them back, sometimes after fistfights with kids—or adults—who felt *proprietary* over what they had taken so much trouble to bring so far away. Rewarding themselves after each mission, he and Nick, with English muffins at the zinc counter of French's Coffee Shop, the craters and crevices in the muffin brimming with melting butter. An English or an order of mashed potatoes and gravy, if he was really hungry, both less than fifty cents.

"What's the Southern word for English muffin?" he asked Robby.

"Cow turd," Robby said.

"Roger English muffin, man," Chris said. "Get some."

He opened the door to Randy's. Ridge thought he saw a flicker of doubt in Robby's eyes, a hesitation before he walked in; the hum of conversation, the laughter and tossed you-alls, dying down to whispers and then silence, as they strutted back to an empty booth where Ridge's ass naturally caught the section of the vinyl cushion patched with duct tape. He and Robby on one side of the table, Chris and Anton on the other. They each looked at the laminated menus, Randy's slogan on the top. Stay the "H" Home. Ridge mouthed the word "hell" and then said it aloud, like a prayer, as if to fill in the blank. But sitting with his friends now he was glad he hadn't stayed the hell home, saw himself pushing an endless line of shopping carts up an eternal slope, right into a sad middle age. He looked further down the menu, seeking the exotic, pondered the word *grits*. Wasn't there a comic book, Sgt. Grit? Meaning stubbornly courageous. Or something, some dust speck you got in your eye. A *grit*. Could a grit be a grunt? Chris and Anton were flipping through the selections on the mini jukebox fastened to the wall. *Soldier Boy, My Boyfriend's Back, It's in His Kiss, Mickey's Monkey, My Girl*, Motown co-existing with Hank Snow and Loretta Lynn. Anton was looking around nervously, as if assessing a new piece of terrain. It was the first time, Ridge realized, they were not eating together in a mess hall or opening C's out in the field. The first time they would have to order and pay for a meal since they put on the uniform.

The waitress was coming towards them. Blonde hair piled up, with a curl falling over her forehead, bee-stung, strawberry lips, creamy skin, firm breasts under a red-checked shirt, and when she turned, tight jeans and a tight ass that he rose to like a pointer. What they were fighting for.

"Serendipitous," Chris said.

"Aesthetic," Anton said.

Robby looked away, fidgeted, reddened, drummed his fingers against the top of the sugar container, Ridge taking it for an attack of the shys, feeling a wave of affection for the big guy. He noticed that the noise level in the restaurant, which had risen slowly since they came in, had fallen again to whispers; some people nudging each other. He thought he understood, recognized the entertainment value of the scene: the GIs and the local girl meeting, cute. The waitress came over to their table. Nothing up close disappointed. She smiled at them warmly, her teeth perfect.

"Your teeth," he said to her, "are perfect."

Chris looked at him with dismay, mouthed: your teeth are perfect?

But her smile didn't fade. "I'm sorry, you all," she said, and nodded at Anton. "We can't serve him in here."

She gestured at a smaller sign, under Stay the "H" home.

A sudden wisdom bloomed on Anton's face, as if he was remembering some vocabulary he should have never forgotten. He nodded at it, grinned tightly, got up. He left the restaurant. The other three stared after him.

"What will you all have," the waitress asked pleasantly.

They sat for a full minute, three white boys staring at the menus in the silence they were now part of. Chris slapped his menu down. "The fuck?" he asked. He rose. Ridge and Robby did also. They had only waited a minute before saying something and joining him. They didn't know then that they would all go to Vietnam in the same outfit and that three of them would survive the war. They didn't know that of the survivors one would eventually take his own life. But they did know that minute would lag between Anton and them for the rest of their lives. By then he had slipped out of the door and was already down the street. Just as he turned the corner, they cleared the door also and tried to follow their friend into America. But he was gone.

THE WAR ON TERROR

SHERIFF RUSSELL HALLAM STILL HAD THE BROAD shouldered, elegantly slim-waisted body that he'd had forty years before when he'd been a young Marine staff sergeant, discharged and come back to a county not quite over the struggles of integration. As a student, before the war, he'd participated in a sit-in and an attempted occupation of this same courthouse building where his office now was, and had been locked up in the same jail he now ran. He hadn't as much won the election last year as been coronated: the former sheriff, Russell's cousin Alex, had retired, and common wisdom had it that people wanted to keep a Hallam in the job. Alex Hallam was white, Russell Hallam black—it was also not uncommon in the county for the old families to have black and white branches. The fact that the name meant more than the color seemed to demonstrate to Hunter how much the county had retained, how much it had changed.

"Afternoon, Uncle Russell," Hunter said. They were not blood relatives. But he had grown up using the term to all the men in his father's circle of Vietnam veterans.

They were meeting today to discuss an article Hunter was writing about a proposed war memorial in the town square; Hallam was the chair of the committee charged with its design. It would contain the names of the county dead from World War II, Korea, Vietnam, and what Hunter had been told would be inscribed on the monument as "The War on Terror," which had already contributed three names. There was already a World War I monument, the names inscribed on it divided in panels labelled "White" and "Colored," and hence a memorial to more than the war. An observation Hunter planned to write in his article.

"Hunter," Hallam said, pronouncing his name as if he were making a statement or identifying a landmark. "Let's eat in my office. Anne fixed us a couple stuffed ham sandwiches."

They walked inside. A metal detector had been set up in the entrance hall. One of Hallam's deputies, Harry Molson, a tall, thin man with a wen on his forehead which Hunter always tried unsuccessfully to avoid staring at, nodded at them, but stopped Hunter when Hallam tried to lead him around the side of the machine.

"Sorry, sheriff. No exceptions."

"Good man," Hallam said. "But reporters like this man?" He pointed at Hunter. "They should go through twice."

Molson grinned at Hunter. "Yes sir. And strip searched."

"You got it. Did you know he writes for *The Enterprise*? Bet you didn't know that star ship had a newspaper."

"I did not know that, sir."

Hunter put his wallet and keys into the little tray.

"I imagine someone like you standing here at the courthouse door when I was arrested—have I ever told you about that, Molson?"

"Many times, sir. Many times."

"Stop being such a kiss up."

Hunter retrieved his things. The sheriff walked around the side.

"You all take care now," Molson said.

In his office, Hallam handed him one of the stuffed ham sandwiches and a cream soda. They ate in silence for a time, Hunter sitting on the other side of the sheriff's gray metal desk. Hunter bit into the sandwich. The dry mustard seed and red pepper that Anne, Hallam's wife, had scored into the ham bit him back. "This is damn good."

Hallam lifted the sandwich. "You did an article on stuffed ham once, didn't you?"

Hunter nodded. The dish was found only in the county: corned ham cooked wrapped in cheesecloth after being scored with deep cuts laced with kale, onions, and other spices and seasonings—the red and black pepper and dry mustard seed Anne Hallam had used—depending on whether it was prepared in South or North County. Hunter had concentrated on the origins of the recipe, brought over from Africa by slaves, the spices supposedly helping to preserve the ham before refrigeration.

"Won a prize for that, I remember. Anne printed it from the on-line edition, taped it on the refrigerator. You should be writing more like that. I enjoyed it."

"Good to hear."

Hallam was staring intently at him. Hunter stared back. The sheriff had carefully pulled at the cloth over his knees when they sat down, maintaining the sharpness of his trouser creases. His uniform was pressed and spotless and polished and he looked twenty years younger than his age. Hallam had been in his father's group of friends, middle-aged men bound by the experience of the war, at ease together, sharing the same excluding vocabulary, if not the same assumptions or politics. Most of them had looked older than their years to Hunter, but like Hallam—except for a requisite gray beard—his father's appearance had stayed frozen in that era also, as if the war of his youth had been some kind of murderous Shangri-La which held the passage of time until you stepped out of its boundaries. That time came for Hunter's father when the cancer began eating him away, his face collapsing to the contours of his skull in that last year, before he'd put the barrel of a gun into his mouth.

"Your dad was a good man," Hallam said. "He was a good friend."

Hunter said nothing. He was unsurprised that Hallam had read his mind.

"Sometimes it seems to me, Hunter, that there is no fucking statute of limitations."

Hallam's anger, the flash of rage in his eyes, the fact he felt somehow charged to shepherd Hunter as if his father's hand rested on his shoulder loosened a flood of grief in Hunter. He turned away, shutting his eyes.

Hallam's cell phone rang. He flipped it open and put it to his ear, suddenly sitting up straight and rigid.

"I'll be right there," he said. He moved the phone away from his ear and was about to close it when whoever was on the other end must have said something. He brought it back up. "No, damn it, keep SWAT and the Staties away. Let's not escalate this unnecessarily." He closed the telephone.

"Sheriff?" Hunter asked.

"Jacob Chappell," Hallam replied, as if it was explanation enough.

• • •

Jacob Chappell had been in the initial invasion of Iraq, back in 2003, as a member of a reconnaissance scout and sniper company. He'd been 22, a graduate of Hunter's high school, and had worked before his enlistment as an auto mechanic for his father, who had come off the family farm and now owned a string of gas stations and repair shops up and down the county. He'd wanted to go to college—something his father saw as unnecessary—and had been attracted by the Army's college funding plan. Hunter didn't know if he ever thought about the politics of the war. A gunner in a criminally under-armored Humvee, he'd found himself continually swiveling his head back and forth like a quizzical bird at the buildings and country on either side of the vehicle, his neck and eyes aching continuously from the movement and the constant strain of trying to see everything at once. One day he spotted a discarded box—the packing crate for a Toshiba television—lying on a traffic island on the airport highway. By the time he'd focused on it and registered it as a possible danger, it had exploded. Parts of the Humvee sliced off a section of the driver's brain and blew it into Chappell's open mouth. He was otherwise untouched and managed to fire his weapon at the place where the Toshiba box had been, his ears ringing, his vision skewed, his mouth reflexively chewing the brain matter that had been blown into his mouth. He registered several robed shapes zigzagging here and there, but by the time his perceptions connected, they were gone.

During the rest of his fifteen months in Iraq—his unit extended three months past their original deployment—he could never get rid of the sensation that his mouth was full and that something he needed to swallow was lodged in his throat. It tasted like raw liver, or sometimes eggs gone slightly bad. His mouth felt filled with bile. He chewed gum. He drank Kool-Aid. But the lump never went down his throat, and the taste never left his mouth. When his unit was rotated back to the States, his enlistment was up, and he came back home and tried to dissolve the blockage in his mouth with Old Bohemian beer, Four Roses whiskey, and local moonshine. When he wasn't speaking to people, his mouth kept working in a continual chewing motion, a tic which got him into several bar room fights, and subsequent arrests by the Sheriff's Department, when drinkers sitting next to him felt mocked or were simply annoyed. His family tried to wrap around him and give him sympathetic listeners: a father and grandfather who'd had their own wars, and their women who had gone through the work of bringing home torn soldiers. They cooked stuffed ham, chicken-fried steaks, ribs, oysters, homemade biscuits, filled Chappell up with their food and the love that went into the food. It seemed to work. He gained twenty-five pounds, met a loving woman, Deidre Renning, who tended bar at the Shore, his favorite place, and gradually felt the presence in his mouth dissolve. He was going to be married next month.

"Then he gets notice that he's been reactivated—he was on Ready Reserve status—and is going to be sent to Afghanistan," Hallam said.

They were driving down a long dirt road to the Chappells' up-county farmhouse. Hallam had left his siren off, not to escalate the situation. No one else seemed to have gotten that idea.

"Shit," Hallam said, and got on his radio again. "Damn it, kill those sirens!" he yelled into the mike.

Chappell had gotten his reactivation notice that morning, via FedEx. As he stared at the words in the message, his mouth seemed to drop down, and then he clamped his lips, holding them tightly together and finally bringing his hand up and trying to pinch his lips between his forefinger and thumb, his eyes darting in panic. He dropped his hand and his mouth began working in a circular motion, as if it had been released. He started kneading his throat, groaning. When he walked back into their bedroom, he was chewing so hard that his fiancée could hear his teeth grinding. Deidre, who told Hallam all this as he was setting up a perimeter around the neat, two-story clapboard house, had rushed over to him, instinctively tried to kiss him, but he'd looked at her in horror, as if, she said, he'd just found out he had a terrible disease and was afraid he would contaminate her. As he pulled away from her, he caught sight of himself in the mirror over their bureau. He pushed her back, went into the living room, and took a shotgun from the rack over the fireplace. He was chewing and swallowing faster and faster, his face red. He came back into the bedroom, sat down on a chair in front of the dresser, and then he pointed the shotgun at it and blew the mirror into shards. Deidre screamed. Chappell took a bottle of Four Roses out from under his nightstand, took a large swig. His chewing caused the liquid to run out of the corners of his mouth. Deidre came towards him, holding her hands out, telling him everything was OK. He pointed the shotgun to his mouth, arm outstretched and thumb around the trigger. Get away from me, he muttered. She backed away and then ran to his parents' house, in a different part of the farm. His grandmother had telephoned the sheriff's department.

Hunter stayed a little ways back, as Hallam conferred with the deputy who'd gone into the house to talk to Chappell. Ron Kirkwood, a tall, thin man with a prominent Adam's apple, was gesticulating excitedly at the sheriff. Kirkwood had recently made noises about running against Hallam in the next election; other deputies had come to Hunter and told him about a whispering campaign he'd started within the department and county courthouse—nothing overtly racist, only little jokes, innuendo about unqualified people being placed in positions beyond their competence. Hunter had written another article in his police column about Kirkwood recently; he'd gone to investigate a report about a breaking and entering and had shot the owner's dog, a poodle, claiming it had been about to bite him. The owner, a recent widower who told Hunter the dog had kept him together after his wife's death—"We took care of each other"—was suing the county. Kirkwood was the worst possible person he could think of to confront Chappell.

"Damn it, Russell; he pointed that gun in my face, told me to get out of his house."

"Sheriff Hallam."

Kirkwood frowned. "*Sheriff* Hallam," he said, somehow making it into a curse.

"Calm down, Deputy. Are all the other family members out of the house?"

"Yes. *Sheriff* Hallam."

"Where are they?"

"At his parents' house. Over the rise."

Hallam turned to one of the other deputies. "You get his grandmother ready to come here, talk to him. She's the calmest of that bunch. But not yet. I'll radio you."

He looked around. Chappell's house was surrounded by open fields and some woodlands. "He's not a threat to anyone. Except himself."

Kirkwood's face reddened. "He damn well threatened me. He can't be allowed to get away with that."

"Did he have another attack poodle, Kirkwood?" Hunter asked.

Kirkwood spun on him. "The fuck are you doing here? Who's the asshole who allowed this asshole on scene?"

"That asshole would be me, Deputy," Hallam said. "Mr. Reed is the media coverage. In fact, he might be the whole tip of the media iceberg, Deputy, if this situation *dramatizes*. So we are going to do everything properly and calmly and try to talk Mr. Chappell down. Is that clear, Deputy?"

"Absolutely, *sir*," Kirkwood said, his teeth clenched. "That's *affirmative,* sir," he said. Since Hallam's election, some deputies were using the word whenever they could, dropping their voices and adding the whispered word "action," afterward. Everyone suspected the usage was started by Kirkwood. He didn't add those words now, but Hunter heard it in his tone. So did Russell Hallam.

"Go sit in your car, Kirkwood. Don't move. Don't do anything."

"Sir, I . . ."

"Go."

He went. Hallam turned to Hunter. "And you'll keep your damn mouth shut and stay out of the way. Is that clear?"

"Yes sir."

He looked at the house again. "Déjà vu all over again,'" he muttered. He shook his head. "Fuck."

He unbuckled his gun belt and handed it to Cal James, one of the other deputies, a sergeant.

"Is that wise, Russ? His wife said he had more shotguns, and at least one .30 caliber in the house, and we know he knows how to use them. We could get more backup in here."

"Cal, the guy is suicidal and there's no one else around here but us chickens. The only call I want you to make is to the shrink: get her out here. Don't. I repeat, Do Not, call in SWAT. We'll talk to him and we'll wait and we'll contain the situation, for as long as it takes. That's all we'll do."

"The Staties will want in."

"They're the last people I want here. Has the land line been re-routed?"

"Yes sir."

"Does he have a cell phone?"

"Yes sir."

"OK, then get your guys around the house, but keep them back at a distance. It's important that Mr. Chappell doesn't feel trapped."

"I understand."

"Say it."

"Sir?"

"Say why it's important to keep everybody at a distance."

"We don't want Mr. Chappell to feel trapped."

"I couldn't have said it better. Now let me have the telephone."

Another deputy handed Hallam the receiver, and he held it to his ear. It must have been ringing already.

"Hello, Mr. Chappell. This is Sheriff Hallam. I'd like to talk to you."

Hallam squinted his eyes, as if straining to hear the response.

"Sir, could you repeat that. I couldn't quite understand."

He stood still, clamping the phone to his ear. There was a bang and one of the windows of the house shattered.

The deputies lying in the field to the left and right of the house raised their guns. Kirkwood came out of his car holding a shotgun. He pointed it at the house. Hallam turned on him, snarling.

"Get the fuck back in the car, Kirkwood. Someone take that gun from him. And everyone calm down. He wasn't aiming at anyone. Look at the angle."

The top of the window had been blown out, but the bottom half of the glass, its edge jagged, was untouched. Chappell must have pointed the gun into the air.

Hallam went over to the car and took out a megaphone. James handed him a small, cigarette lighter-sized recorder. He switched it on and put it into his breast pocket. He buttoned the pocket and cautiously walked up to the front porch, his hands in the air. He went up the steps. They creaked loudly under his weight.

"Mr. Chappell," he called. "I'm coming in. Please don't shoot me."

He twisted the front doorknob. It turned. Hunter heard James, standing next to him, inhale sharply. Then realized he had also. The silence seemed to stretch into minutes, though it could only have been a few seconds. Hallam pushed the door open and went inside.

• • •

As Hallam enters, he passes a hallway bathroom, and can see the mirror in it had been shattered also. Looking at it, seeing his own shattered face, he has the sense that Chappell is killing himself in pieces, working his way to his real flesh. Chappell is sitting on the couch in the living room, dressed only in a pair of jockey shorts. Hallam can see fresh cuts and scratches on his chest, shoulders, and belly, overlaying scar tissue from older wounds. Chappell's body hair maps his body out in patches, as if clumps of it had been torn out. He is chewing rapidly, his teeth grinding, and the hand that isn't on the shotgun is kneading his throat, as if working a lump that Chappell can feel but that Hallam can't see.

"Mind if I sit down?" Hallam says softly.

He doesn't wait for a reply but sits across from Chappell, in a straight-backed wooden chair. Chappell points the barrel of the shotgun at him and Hallam realizes belatedly that he does not know what he is going to say. He has thought to appeal to Chappell as a fellow veteran, but now fears bringing in his own experiences would just sound patronizing or judgmental to Chappell. Some of his own deputies, young veterans, had become defensive when he had tried to find a commonality with them by telling war stories; he remembers later overhearing one, Jessica Whitten, saying to Bernie Molson that Hallam was *showing off his battle dick*. It had been the way his generation had reacted to World War II vets; the Vietnam veterans, the stories of the Greatest Generation implied, had not fought a *real* war, and anyway had lost their war.

What comes into his mind now is a sequence of photos from the battle for Hill 881. He had seen the images in a book of photographs from the war that a clueless county commissioner had given him as a birthday gift. It had sat on a table for months like a trap, and when he finally opened it, those photos had struck him like a blow between his own eyes. The photographs formed a tetraptych. In the first, a corpsman kneels next to a fallen Marine, pressing his chest to perform CPR;

they are on the steep, blasted side of the hill, splintered trees around them. In the second, he has lowered his head to try to breathe into the fallen man's mouth. In the third, the corpsman looks up the hill, his mouth open in anguish and anger, at the failure of his craft, at the irredeemable loss. No one has been saved. In the fourth, there is only the fallen man and the feet of the corpsman as he continues up that fire-swept hill. Hallam had been on that hill. He remembered the photographer, a slight, young French woman; his helicopter—Hallam had been a door gunner—had dropped her off. Maybe they had dropped off that corpsman and that Marine as well. What was her name? Levoy? Leroy? The Marines at the LZ, before they were lifted in, had made the usual round-eye pussy comments; after the battle though anyone who talked about her that way, he'd been told, would get punched in the face. She was one of them. She had her battle dick. Leroy, that was it. Cathy. Catherine. Seeing her photographs gave him the sensation of something extracted physically from his own mind, suddenly solidifying forms drawing in repressed, particulate memories to themselves like filings to a magnet, filling in shapes he'd tried hard to forget.

Chappell is staring at him. Not expectantly, not waiting for him to speak. Just sitting. His finger still on the trigger of the shotgun. The Humvee in which he had been blown up had been so inadequately armed, Hallam recalls, that the men in his unit had chipped in to buy scrap metal they rigged as side and underneath armor. He can speak to him about that, share an indignant rage at the betrayal of trust in authority that knit across a generation their common experience of war. On 881, after the battle, he had seen Marines lying dead next to their stripped down, piece-of-shit new M-16s, jammed in the middle of the battle. What rushes to him now is not so much a memory as the emotion that connected to the memory; the dead he helped drag onto the deck of his helicopter looking like nothing more than a heaped pile of disregarded equipment and uniforms, as if it had been those accoutrements, the same shell of cloth and leather stained with red mud that contained and defined his mortal form, more than their shredded flesh that had contained their living souls.

Chappell hasn't stopped staring. As far as Hallam can tell, he hadn't even blinked. But his body is rocking slightly.

He takes a deep, shuddering breath. He is soaking wet, the sudden intrusive memory of those photographs, not the battle itself, but the way it had bled through those images into his present lie, seizing him from inside like something pinching his heart and lungs, and he thinks maybe both of them will never leave this house.

"It got," he says to Chappell, "under my skin. The war. I built a fence between me and what I thought my life was supposed to be. The me that came back. You know what my daddy said a good fence should be? 'Pig strong and horse high.' Your granddaddy ever tell you that, this farm? It was what I figured I had to do. But you know, my wife made me tell it to her. Tell her everything. She was going to hear it, she was going to take that death under her own skin. That's what she told me, that's what she did. She made me feel I was not a *leper*, do you understand? I've met your fiancée, I know your family, son. They know you; they love you. They will listen to you and they will understand you and they will, they do, love you. That love will bring you back, I know it will."

He has closed his eyes while speaking these last bromides, as if shutting himself off from the falsity, the happy, movie-of-the-week ending phoniness of his own words, and when he opens them he sees that Chappell is rocking back and forth on the couch, his mouth working faster, his eyes darting back and forth like trapped animals. He picks up a note pad from the table next to him and writes something on it. He hands it to Hallam.

They didnt make you go back, the note reads.

Hallam closes his eyes, nods. There is nothing he can say to that.

Chappell takes the pad back, scribbles on it again. *I dont want to hurt nobody. Just leave me be.*

"Son," Hallam starts. And then feels he has been swallowed by his own nightmares, conjured up by the memory he has just unwrapped as if he were peeling off his skin to bring it out again. The sound now drowning out his words is the familiar staccato drum beat of helicopter rotors, blowing their great wind down on the roof over his head.

• • •

As soon as Hallam had gone into the house, Hunter saw Kirkwood get out of his car, staring towards the door with an intensity of hatred that sent a chill up Hunter's neck. The deputy stood like that for a moment, and then began to pace back and forth, filled with a barely suppressed energy. As soon as he went back into the car, and picked up his handset, Hunter knew what he was doing.

"Sheriff Hallam said he didn't want any outside agencies."

Kirkwood stood up, holding the handset.

"I need you to back off."

The more he covered the police beat, the more Hunter had come to hate that phrasing, picked up from cop shows and now used by every cop he knew.

"Sheriff Hallam *needs* you to not escalate this situation."

"I need you to step away from the car."

"What about my needs?"

"Just get the fuck away from the car, Reed."

"Don't make that call." Some of the other deputies had gathered around them.

Kirkwood took his gun out of its holster and pointed it at Hunter.

"Are you shitting me," Hunter said.

"Jim," Frank Ng, one of the other deputies started. Kirkwood frowned and contorted his forehead. Hunter saw his own face reflected in the silver lens of his aviator's sunglasses.

"Turn around," Kirkwood said. "Put your hands on top of the car and spread your legs."

He seized Hunter's shoulder, spun him around and kicked his legs apart. Hunter didn't resist. He sat behind the latticed metal that separated suspect from officer and listened to Kirkwood call the State Police and the sheriffs' departments of two neighboring counties.

When Hallam came out of the house, the helicopter dipped low again. He glared at it and then looked around. When Hunter saw him staring at the cruiser, he tried to stand up as much as he could, to indicate his handcuffed hands. Hallam pushed his face forward, his mouth hanging open in astonishment, and then clamped shut in rage, the emotions as apparent as if they'd been labeled under illustrations in some psych textbook. Kirkwood looked in the rearview mirror, and then adjusted it, squared away his hat, bringing the brim down nearly to his eyebrows, straightened his sunglasses and got out of the driver's seat. Hallam had closed the distance between them and was standing nose to nose with Kirkwood. He was soaked in sweat and was as close to losing control as Hunter had ever seen him. He yanked Kirkwood's gun out of its holster, put it in his own pocket. When he opened his mouth, the roar of the helicopter rotors seemed to blast out of it, the machine nearly on top of them. Leaves spun around Hallam and Kirkwood and struck the back window to which Hunter was pressing his face. As the aircraft continued into its circle, a shotgun blast sounded from the house again, along with the tinkle of shattering glass.

Hunter watched the scene transform into the nightmare vision that Hallam had tried to prevent. Inevitably. It was the moment in a dream when what you fear will happen comes into your perception and causes that very thing. Sirens blared from all sides, as cruisers came tearing down the road to the farmhouse and two of the other access roads, raising a fine yellow dust that hung in the air throughout the afternoon. Two jeeps came tearing over the drought-dry fields, raising large yellow clouds of dust. SWAT teams from the county and two neighboring counties arrived in armored vehicles. They swarmed around yelling to each other before settling into a perimeter around the house. A sharpshooter in a black bullet proof vest and a plastic-visored helmet crusted with cyclopean lenses moved up behind the faux well half-way up the lawn; Hunter could see others climbing trees in the copse of woods near the barn. Three more were in the barn loft. He wondered if anyone was coordinating all this fire power. If they all started shooting, Hunter figured, they would be torn to pieces in the crossfire.

Frank Ng walked over to him and unlocked the handcuffs. As Hunter rubbed his wrists, he heard the roar of another motor and looked down the road. A Peacekeeper vehicle—it seemed to him a kind of ungainly armored jeep—pulling up, making a rattling noise, like BBs in a tin can. The State Police were here. The Peacekeeper was painted black also—what was the impulse, Hunter wondered, for SWAT units to use that color, feed every right-wing Waco nut's fantasy of fleets of black helicopters sent by the ZOG to take their hunting rifles? His mind was running all over the place. So as not to be here. He felt a sudden sick apprehension. He rubbed his wrists, and trotted to keep up with Hallam, who was playing whack-a-mole with the different commands who had shown up and were each setting up according to their own plans, with no attempt at coordination. Hallam ran over to one side of the yard, got the sheriff from the neighboring county in tow, ran over to the other and got the next sheriff, and then led them over to the barn, where Tom Cavanaugh, the Staties commander, was standing. Cavanaugh had a megaphone in one hand, and a blueprint diagram of the small house pinned on a table. Hunter saw one of the State SWAT guys, dressed in their Darth Vader-like armor, standing next to him and nodding as Cavanaugh pointed to the map as if he were directing the Battle of the Bulge. He frowned when he saw Hunter.

"Reed, what the hell are you doing here?"

He resisted the urge to say, "my job." There were already too many people here who thought they were in a movie.

It was late afternoon now. The helicopter had mercifully flown away, perhaps to refuel, and the air was suddenly silent. The red paint of the barn, slapped over weathered wood that showed through in places like gray skin, the green of the locust leaves flipping up and showing their metal-colored undersides, all seemed exaggerated, each a picture of itself. Cavanaugh made him back off a little, but as the men spoke, Hunter edged forward to eavesdrop.

"What the hell do you mean, *quick kill?*" Hallam was saying. If he were white, Hunter thought, his face would be mottled red with anger. It was manifesting itself now in the tightness of his lips, the cords of muscle standing out on his neck.

"Russell, calm down," Rachel Stuyvesant, one of the other sheriffs, said to him. "We're just talking all the contingencies we need to keep in mind."

"The man is armed and dangerous," Seth Mahoney, the other sheriff said.

"Armed and dangerous," Hallam said, shaking his head. "Whoo-ee, Seth."

Cavanaugh shook his head. "Why are you being so obstructive, Russell?"

"Ob-struc-tive." Hallam shook his head. "Whoo-ee."

"Please," Cavanaugh said, pained.

"OK, great," Hallam said. "Look, gentlemen and lady," a nod to Stuyvesant, "the ones armed and dangerous here are us. The only person Chappell is a danger to is himself. We can lower that risk if we keep a low profile, talk to him, bring him out. He's drinking too. He might pass out any minute."

"I disagree," Cavanaugh said. "Chappell is an armed and trained combat soldier. If he gets loose."

"Gets loose?" Hallam interrupted. "Crazed Veteran Runs Amok. Is that the picture you're painting here, Cavanaugh?"

Stuyvesant turned to him angrily, her eyes narrowed, her normally calm and placid face twitching with anger. She opened her mouth to say something.

At that instant, the firing started.

Later, Hunter would remember it that way, as if whatever Stuyvesant was about to say had instigated the wrath of fire that poured down onto that muted, broken soldier who had so impotently armed himself against the forces insisting on his return to battle.

Three of the State Police were standing behind the faux-well, shooting tear gas canisters at the house. They smashed through the front windows, shattering the glass in the two windows that had not been blasted out by Chappell's shotgun. The Peacekeeper pulled up parallel to the door, as if to block it. From where Hunter stood, he could see three other men run to the side of the house, paste something on the vinyl siding, and run back.

More shotgun blasts came from the house. Hunter could see pellets hitting the windows of one of the police cruisers. Some starred the glass, but most pinged off.

Hallam snatched the megaphone from Cavanaugh. "This is Sheriff Hallam. Hold your fire. I repeat, hold your fire." He pushed the megaphone in the direction of the car, shouted at the other three. "Look at that windshield. He's only shooting bird shot."

As if to reinforce his assessment, a voice came from the house. "Le' me be! I ain't gonna hurt nobody!"

They were the clearest words Chappell had spoken that day. They were drowned in the fusillade.

Hunter, his heart thudding in his chest and then galloping into a staccato roll, ran towards the house. He had no idea what he was going to do when he got there. Hallam told him later that he had spun around and stuck his arms out, as if he was going to catch the bullets.

To his chagrin, it was Kirkwood who tackled him and got him out of the line of fire.

All he remembered clearly is how, afterwards, when they took Chappell's body from the house, his grandmother had pushed aside a deputy and kissed the dead boy's forehead.

And his grandfather had spit in Russell Hallam's face.

"Nigger," he said.

AMERICAN
GRASS

I OPEN MY EYES. THE OLD MAN, I REALIZE, IS PINCHING me. Crab scurries over my thighs and boobs. Let him; I've paid more for rides. *Chao ong,* he says to me, almost under his breath, like leaving out a little piece of bait. Getting the words wrong anyway. Hello mister. Little wire pig bristles of hair clumped inside his ears. Shirt buttoned up to his neck wattles. Me looking at him thinking the same thing he's probably thinking looking at me: *They're everywhere.*

I turn my head and let my forehead tap tap into the cool glass, watching what flows by the window. *Ma,* the word for ghost, drifts into my mind and I play with that, play with being Ma, her wandering soul blown into me. My own lost Mama Ma, a restless VC ghost, blown over here to the World. Loose in the enemy capital. I can see the big white dome now just like the pictures. We drive around it and down a wide street. He slows down, the car, not his hands, his eyes half-closed and I see a street sign, the one I've been looking for. I finger walk my own hand over to his crotch, the inky, dinky spider . . . grab and twist. He screams and slams on the brakes and I'm out the door and gone, running out of a shit storm of horns and brakes and screams. Thanks for the lift. Exit Kiệt. *Chao ong,* motherfucker.

After a minute I force myself to slow down and walk calmly along the sidewalk, trying to look part of it all, a fish in the sea of people. Just like Ma would have done. I flow with the tourists, seeing some vets among them now, wearing their ribbons and badges and wheelchairs, some of them bony and eaten away, their faces like sticks chewed on the inside by insects, hollowed and caving in; others bulging and oozing out of the gaps between the straining buttons on their old fatigues like that's all they got to hold them from melting off into nothing. All of them turning and staring at me in my black clothes and sandals and VC eyes. Then I see that all the vendor trucks along the street are manned by VC homies too, selling hot dogs and eggrolls and copper Washington Monuments and Snow-Globes (turn them over and shake them and napalm falls on a thatched roof village). And t-shirts saying *tough shit yeah we're here now*, their Vietnam faces squinting at me like who's this dust? The kind of cool I want to learn someday, learn how to look through people like they're air behind themselves. Down I go, past them, past the white, columned buildings, down alongside the long pool. Seeing myself a black spoiling speck against all that gleaming white. This skinny VC girl on the run, weeks into the jungle on nothing but a handful of moldy rice and stinky fish and burning hate. The last and furthest point of the 1990 Tet Offensive.

I see the Word in front of me on a sign, like it had leapt out of my head. Word for a place so angry and stubborn it means the same as a war. I follow the sidewalk down and there it is.

And here I am.

I walk closer. On the grass near the Wall is a bamboo cage, under a sign: *AMERICANS ARE STILL HELD CAPTIVE BY ASIA: POW'S NEVER HAVE A NICE DAY.* Inside, a man in a tattered, tiger-stripe flight suit looks at my face, my black clothes, and frowns. His leg is manacled. Nearby, people are clustered in front of the little stands that hold the name books. I know what they are. I know where I am. The sidewalk slants down in front of me to the two wings of the black granite Wall, like they're the opening pages of a book themselves. I wait in line. The books are under plastic, like the plastic they have over salad bars in restaurants, so you can reach and touch but you can't breathe on it or put your face down into it or kiss it or lick it or bite it. 58,108 listed, a woman in a pink mumu dress says, shaking her head. Like she's going to say whoo-ee. I put my hands into the slot under the scratched plastic and turn the pages, skimming the lists of names and ranks and towns and dates and numbers of panels and lines. Like 15E 33. Like a phone book of the dead. What would happen, I go to a phone, try that number? Who'd answer? Not that I know my dad's name. The name they gave me was just something issued. GI Government Issue. I look it up anyway. It isn't there. I look at my face, the enemy's face, floating transparent over the names. GF: Ghost Face. GI: Ghost Issue.

I close the book and start walking down to the Wall. I'm sharp with hunger and clear, the way I get sometimes on the street. On my right, I see the three bronze soldiers, one of them my black daddy, looking in astonishment at me, here. I look away, over at the names. But I can't go down to them. Like being finally touchable real would take them away from me forever.

Three girls are staring at me, giggling, eating eggrolls. Lunch with the dead. Three mall rats in their yuppie kid baggy khaki like the lost expedition of rich bitches. Maybe my age. Two tall blondes and another gook like me, only shorter, squatter; they keep her for amusement. Only now they got me. Wrinkling their noses, looking at my face, my black clothes, this off-brand grrrl ghost. Roll their eyes, whisper. Laughter dribbles, they press it back inside, swallow it.

Me, I'm hungry.

I'm the Tet Offensive, I say to blonde one.

Excuse me?

She's astonished to be addressed by dust.

No.

What is your problem, blonde two says.

You numbah hucken ten.

What are you talking about? The dwarf glares at me, their funny face doll, their dusty pet.

She no speakee, speakee, blonde one says. It's the funniest thing they ever heard, so she says it again.

I'm no seey-seey, I say. You can't see me. I live in tunnels under your stupid fucking lives.

I snatch blonde two's eggroll and begin scarfing it down quickly. Hey, she yells. I see a park ranger, Smokey the Bear hat and all, walking toward us. I start to move. Hey, the dwarf yells; she doesn't want to be left out and throws her eggroll at me. It explodes, a warm burst heart, tiny shrimps and slimy cabbage on my chest. The VC live off the land, Ma tells me. Bonus. I grab it as it slides and off I go.

Ma 'n Kiệt on the run.

No Lie.

I find a little jungly screen of bushes and sit there, eating the burst eggroll and watching the flow of the river until it gets dark. The water crinkles and sparkles in the last light of the sun, and then, so slowly I can't remember when it happens, the color is sucked away and there's only a heavy sliding blackness in front of me, erasing everything, carrying it all away, a scum of moonlight oily and slick on it. A boat goes by, outlined in lights, people eating, dancing on its deck. Music drifts to me. I squint and try to see another boat behind it, people shitting over the side, hanging onto each other, glued together with their own sweat and stink. *Hey! Wait for us!*

I pat my shirt pocket making sure what's left of the other eggroll is still there. A horse whinnies, like this crazy laugh. I hear the clatter of hooves coming closer and then I remember that the cops here sometimes ride horses. I scoot back under the overhang of the bush. Someone has used this nest before, left crumpled cans, a condom hanging on a twig, its little bulb still heavy and swaying. The horse passes so close by I can see its breath push at the lace of leaves and branches over my face, feel the thud of its hooves stomping down near my head. I roll out, scramble to my feet and run, zigzagging into the dark, seeing the horse rearing up out of the corner of my eye. I hear the cop shout. I lie down, black on black, and he gallops by me like a movie. Lying there, I think for a while, motionless, and then I know where to go. Chased by the US fucking cavalry or not.

Only a few people are at the Wall at this time of night, passing like shadows in front of the names, some of them squatting in front of the panels. The MIA cage is empty. I slip in between the bars, slip on the leg manacle, lie down on my back, and try to look like a pile of rags. Or like part of the exhibit. I'm home.

I take the eggroll out of my shirt pocket, nibble on it a little to calm myself, then put it down. Someone goes by, looks in at me, catches his breath, moves on. Over to my left I can see the Wall. The names faint lines in the moonlight, scratches on a dark mirror. Shadows move along in front of them, touching and patting them with pale hands. I draw my knees up and put my face against them and try not to think. Then try to think about other things. Try not to think about the Wall. The Wall on the Mall. I think about taking Ma shopping in a real mall. Like the one where I hung out a few days, where the old man picked me up? Showing that to Ma. Dear dead never seen Ma. Dead in a world of thatch and trees and rice paddies and all that shit. How would she see all that concrete and glass? Like a scaly dragon lying in the sun? A mouth door that hisses open as we come near. A cool gray gullet that swallows us. Looking up at the squares of mirrors in the ceiling, seeing my long black hair, my slit eyes, my black clothes. *Attention shoppers, there are two VC loose in the Mall.* Cold dead air touches Ma's cold dead skin, *Eat,* a sign tells us. You bet. Check out all these choices, Ma. What'll it be? *Wok N Eggroll, Steak N Fries, Bagels R Us, TCBY. This Can't Be You.* Hard light shines through Ma's wavy form reflected in the store display windows. Welcome to the World, Ma. Which World? *Mattress World. Video Empire. Computer Universe. Ghosts R Us.* People staring at the mannequins except in one window where they're staring at a woman who's pretending to be a mannequin, crying out with mean delight if they can get her to make human movements and I want to kill them all, waste them all. *Fifteen-Year-Old Viet Vet Ghost Runs Amok. Possessed by VC Soul, Claims Deranged Teen.* Ma gliding cool as can be past stacked rows of TV screens in a window, a black-pajamaed form flowing screen to screen and I turn to try and catch her but she's gone, with only my funny, missed-up nothing face there, Kiệt Keisha's dust face staring back at me on screen after screen.

Someone pinches me.

I'm at the Wall.

In front of me a skinny white man with thin patchy red hair. Only where he's lost it on his head, it grows like fox fur on his arms and cheeks. This I see plainly, in the light from the moon. Hair so red and thin it makes the white scalp under it whiter, like bone. Eyes gleaming. Bony face smudged with dirt, camouflage fatigues stiff and stinking. Bony white hand reaching through the bars of the cage. Only not a hand. One of those metal claw pincher thingies they give you instead of hands. He's attached chicken bones onto the two pinchers. Cool. I hope they're chicken bones.

Hey, little gook, he says, that's my gig.

Just Homeless, I think as I unshackle and scramble out quickly, still shuddering. He goes in, sits down, and slips on the leg manacle. Both hands, I see, are the same. I reach back in through the bars. He slaps my hand. The metal and bone hurts.

I left my eggroll, I say.

He picks it up, sniffs it, looks me up and down, recognizing me. You hungry, Mizz Cong, he asks. Hungry for the food of the East. Hey kid—want an eggroll?

He puts his claw through the bars, offering it me, but snatches it back when I reach. Be polite, Mizz Charlie. Bites off half, pushes the rest back through the bars, watches me. Beats out a rhythm with his rattley claws.

Mizz Charles
Sucking on mah eggroll
Sucking on my brain box
Asken for a bagel lox
Asken for a sweet n sour
Asken for another hour

So what they call you, Mizz Charles, he asks.

Nothing.

Yeah? Me too. Used to be Skip. I come from this place, see, every-body called Skip, Buzz, Chip, right? Like noises. Like nothing. So now I'm just Missing. Oozed out between the names. The space between the lines. Like this little red toadstool, right? Pops out, swells up, grows. This polyp. So come on. What's your name?

Lucy, I say, lie. No way I'll name my soul to this one.

Juicy Lucy? So you're here too, huh Luce? Came on over. Followed me back. So how do you like the World? Gotta be better than that shithole, right? Hey, you know something, Lucy? Know what I heard? From the odd wandering monk or two? All that country over there that was scarred up, destroyed by orangeade and napalm and stuff—it's all growing out again. Only instead of jungle or bamboo or good paddy land, it's all coming up in grass. Tough grass. The gook farmers hate it. They can't weed it—too deep-rooted and the roots tangle up under the ground, strangle other plants. They call it American Grass, Mizz Charles. It grows everywhere. At night it comes into the villages, creeps up the walls of thatched hootches, penetrates, makes strange changes. It slips into the body orifices of sleeping farmers and their wives. Morning comes, they wake up with this urge to develop, buy stuff, name their kid Lucy.

They love Lucy, I say.

How you know that show? How old you, fifteen, sixteen? You don't remember nothin', do you? Got no idea. Got on the boat, got off the boat. Got welcomes with open arms. Meanwhile, me, I never got back.

I'm missing. I never had a parade. Nary a muster. Thing was I was afraid to come back, see, 'cause I heard about all those spitters, right? I heard there were spitters everywhere. Gobbers, hawkers, oyster spewers waiting for me at airports, train stations, Greyhound bus terminals, ferries, ox cart junctions, any public transportation whatsoever. Even at home. Town mayor, county commissioners, cops, even Ma, Pa, granny, little sis, dog, the whole extended family coming out to hawk one on me. Figured wherever I went, let me tell you, Lucy, things would get wet and drippy. Screw that. Better to stay missing. Otherwise, people would treat me just like I was a gook. Like I'd developed these epican-thic folds, see?

He pulls his eyes narrow with the two tips of his claws. Me, you, same-same, right?

No way. Not me. I'm Vietnam grass, man. You touch me and I'm coming in, right through your pores, your asshole. I'll come in while you're sleeping and I'll fill your throat, my little tendrils wrap around your voice box so you can't scream. My roots'll push into your lungs and stomach, under your skin, wrap around your guts, inside your eyeballs, your balls-balls—you try and pull them out and you'll pull out your insides, man, your heart.

He stares at me. You're the love of my life, he says. No shit. Hey, Juicy Charlie, don't worry; I could be your daddy, right?

You ain't nobody's daddy. Get out of my head, man. You can't do that, go in, pull shit out of people's heads.

He grins, scratching his chest with his pinchers, digging into the skin. You met your real daddy, what you do?

Fuck a whole buncha daddies.

He throws back his head and laughs. Like a stream of clicks pouring out of his mouth, like there's a mass of chickens bulging in his throat. Don't say nothing else funny, I tell myself.

How 'bout your mama? You remember her?

Ma means ghost, you know that? I ask.

Tip of the ectoplasmic iceberg, Luce. You guys got all kinds of ghosts, good and bad, lots a' names. But the bad ones—*oo-ee,* Lu-cy. Wandering spirits, people killed with violence, with the old extreme prejudice, never had altars built for them. Listen, I know; I got one a them too. No shit. You know the name of mine? Willy Peter. That's White Phosphorous to all you civilian Fucking New Guy Charlies. Will's this luminous white cloud, all the little particles bury themselves in your flesh, burn like hell, melt the flesh right off your bones. Cover him with mud and the burn stops. But the minute the mud dries, cracks, air gets in—he's baaaack. Burning right down to the bone. Like memory. Know what I mean, kiddo? Get some air on it, it *burns,* baby, burns baaad. Old Willy Peter. He waves at the Wall. But you guys are smart, see, you build altars for those wandering souls. Like a shelf, they can come rest. Like a Wall they can hang on. You gotta build them an altar, so they won't wander around, fuck with the living. Come once a year, light some joss sticks, say their names. Say, hi guys, how's it hanging? Show 'em you care. Give 'em an egg roll. He points again at the Wall. You think any of this is an accident, Miz Charlie? It's like it came after us. Like you did. Since when Americans build altars for wandering souls, come here, talk to them, leave offerings? Flowers, wreaths, photos, cigarettes, teddy bears. Just like the altars over there where they died. Just like you come here, kiddo. Like you want to rest, come in, stay with us for a while, little guy . . .

I run. From his claws reaching through the bars. From the part of me that wants to seep back in through the bars like a tendril, curl up, stay with him right there in the cage.

I run down to the black V, his cricket laughter clicking louder and louder behind me. The black Wall folds around me. I go down, down, in, in, the Wall growing taller and taller. The moonlight is bright and I can see my reflection flowing wavy around the white shocks of the names. The names give little tugs and pinches at my insides. Spider scurries. My Ma's name is my face reflected in the polished stone. My daddy writes his name on my forehead but whenever I try to see it another name nudges it and replaces it. A murmur follows me, the names clucking in disapproval. I lean my forehead against the cool stone, the names stitching themselves to it, licking me like stupid fucking puppies, take me home, take me home. I push my whole body against the Wall. Daddy daddy daddy daddy daddy 58,108 times. A cloud covers the moon and I disappear into the black Wall. Black into black. I push like I'm pushing into the cold skin of water. It seizes me, my nose and ear openings and eyes and all my hollows filling with black. Disappearing.

I tear myself away and move up towards the light, feeling myself being named and born out of the black living wedge of the dead.

EXTRACT

A RED CIRCLE GLOWING JUST IN FRONT OF HIS CON-
sciousness. He fought to hold onto sleep, knowing he would lose. The
red circle grew larger and brighter, and he resentfully felt the sleep leave
him. He blinked his eyes open and stared into the Duty NCO's flashlight. "Get that thing out of my eyes," he said sharply.

The light lowered slightly. "It's time," the Duty whispered. His voice
was low with pre-dawn reverence.

The gunner hunched under the rough green blanket, feeling some
sand that had been caught in the sag of his cot grate into his spine. He
squinted at the Duty, making him into a dark train locomotive silhou-
ette, his flashlight the menacing headlamp. He saw something white
extend from the dark form and he opened his eyes fully. A clipboard.
"Initial it," the Duty said. "I ain't got all morning." The gunner took
the offered pencil stub and initialed the piss-call sheet next to his typed
name and the time. The Duty, absolved of any more responsibility,
nodded at him and left the hootch.

He sat up. He saw Sam standing at the other end of the hootch, his naked
black bulk lit in flickering red by a candle. Sam pulled on his flight suit and
took his mess gear down from a nail, clanging it, indifferent to the sleeping
shapes lumped on their cots. The gunner glanced around at the interior of
the hootch. Ten evenly lined cots between bare tin walls. It looked like a skid
row transient hotel that had somehow trapped and held onto its guests. A
place for old men with spit on their shirts, he thought angrily.

Sam finished dressing and walked over to his cot. "You gonna get some chow," he asked.

"Naw, don't guess so. I'll meet you at the flight line."

"Up to you, man." Sam squinted at him. "You sure you're OK?"

"Yeah, fine. Just I had some kinda dream and it's still hanging on me, you know?"

"Yeah?" Sam shifted on his feet and his metal cup clanged against the metal tray he was dangling from a piece of hanger wire. "Alright. Catch you later," he said, then hesitated.

"Listen, 'tenant DeLeon said to be sure and get .50's for the bird, 'count of we're going North. Don't let the armory stick you with no M-60's."

"Sure thing," he said, and Sam turned and left.

He lit his candle and sat naked on the edge of his cot. He rubbed his face repeatedly and looked around him. After a while he got up and started to get dressed.

The sun had just started to rise from the South China Sea. It barely lit the flight line, just turning the nighttime black into gray and not yet bothering with colors.

He had finished struggling the heavy .50's into the armatures set behind the open front ports of the Sea-Knight. He enjoyed the feel of heavy metal slipping well into position but hated to feel the sweat start and spoil the long cooling of the night.

Now he stood in front of the Operations tent, a hot metal cup filled with black coffee stinging the small cuts in his greased hands. He looked out at the helicopter mat. The dawn light made the CH-46 helicopters look like a neatly lined platoon of sinister grasshoppers. He sipped at his coffee and let his mind wander with the sun's rise.

He looked at Sam, up on the green spine of number seven, peering at the engine. Looking head-on at the helicopter, he could see the barrels of both guns sticking out of the side ports.

The pilots began spilling out of the briefing tents. He gulped down the rest of his coffee and ran out to the helicopter. Sam climbed down and stood beside him, wiping his hands on his hips. They stood together and waited for the officers. DeLeon was slightly in front of his co-pilot, a new guy named Anderson, who scurried chubbily to keep up with him. First Lieutenant DeLeon sported a bushy, slightly off-reg gunfighter's mustache; he walked behind it as if it were a separate entity he was presenting to the sunrise.

When they reached the helicopter, Anderson climbed up to check Sam's pre-flight as DeLeon briefed the crewmen.

"Sir, you said something 'bout going to the 'Z again," Sam asked. "Yesterday?"

"'Fraid so, Corporal Deeson," DeLeon said, and then smiled. "We have an extract up there, a recon team."

The gunner was staring at the Lieutenant's face. The sickness he had been feeling all morning was bursting in strong bubbles in his gut. The face seemed to him to be strangely translucent, almost gaseous behind the curved black bar of the mustache, as if it were only the anchoring hair to keep it from being blown away, DeLeon's lips were moving, rubbery and androidlike; the gunner watched them in sick fascination, not hearing the words coming out. Sweating heavily, the sweat spreading over his skin like a dirty film of soot. We're dropping some passengers at Phu Bai, then continuing to Dong Ha, DeLeon was saying, his voice distant. They look like nylon, those mustache hairs, the gunner thought, like each nylon hair was glued separately into each gaping little pore above the officer's lip. He could feel the soft weight of those nylon hairs encircling his skin and snaring him, weblike, to the lieutenant. He felt lifeless, a small particle carried helplessly on DeLeon's words. He saw the lips moving and noticed dully the ridge of yellow cottage-cheesy smudge between the gum lines and the teeth. More teeth showed suddenly as DeLeon grinned. We'll be passing over some of those fucking villages; we take any fire, don't wait for my permission to return it. Waste them. Don't worry about women or kids. Littledinksgrowintobigcong. Use those fifties.

Must come with pubic hair then, this cong.

The gunner watched as the pilot climbed into the helicopter. He felt detached from the entire scene, somewhere beneath it.

"You still with us," Sam asked.

"Yeah."

"No shit. Let's get a hat. Let's get some fresh air, man."

• • •

The barrel of his machine gun bisected a piece of blue sky and hung threateningly over the landscape. He looked out over it. The country north of Hue had broken out in thousands of Vietnamese grave mounds. They flew over stretches of sand and graves and then shining brown mirrors of paddyland. The helicopter's shadow covered and uncovered some cone-hatted farmers. They didn't look up.

A village was coming up, green cauliflower trees and brown huts making an island in the expanse of the flooded rice fields. He leaned forward as DeLeon brought the helicopter to tree-top level. The maneuver was supposed to confuse snipers, the roar of the engine startling them, and the helicopter gone before they could get it together.

They were moving fast, maybe at 100 knots, yet the gunner's gaze fell and wrapped itself in the doorway of one hut. For a suspended moment he could see the doorway as clear and still as if he were walking up to it on the ground. The brown-yellow thatch of the hut stood out starkly against the green around it, the contrast making it seem more solid and substantial. He felt a sharp twinge of connection to the hut, its solidity filling the hollowness of his sickness. A woman was squatting on her heels in front of the door, absorbed in mixing something in a bowl. He imagined he could see her smiling, her teeth betel-nut blackened, at the naked child playing next to her in the yellow dirt.

They were passing over the village and the passage tore at him. He felt their transience at that moment. They were just a loud noise and a green flash in the sky, gone too soon to be remarked on. Their loudness was only, after all, a child's cry to be noticed, a child's threat if ignored.

The grasshoppers were scattered all over the ground at Dong Ha. They began circling in and he opened the breech of the .50 and took the ammo belt out of the gun. He was startled by a sharp blow on the back of his helmet and turned fast to see Sam glaring at him. The crew chief swore and threw the belt back into position. The gunner nodded at him and slammed the breech back down, then cocked the gun, twice, stayed behind it as they landed. DeLeon's voice was crackling in his ears over the intercom; just hop out and refuel, the crackling said, we're going right out.

They disconnected their gunners' belts and intercom wires, and went out the front hatch. He ran and got the fuel line as Sam opened the tank. He inserted the hose and squeezed the nozzle trigger, letting the fuel pour in. Sam was shaking his head. "Sorry I hit you," he yelled over the engine noise. "You should know better to unload 'fore we touch down here. This ain't Danang."

"Yeah; sorry, Sam," he said, meaning it. "I don't know where my head's at today." Sam shrugged. The gunner felt the fuselage of the helicopter jerk up, full, and he stopped the flow. He ran back with the hose, then back to the plane, entering and buttoning the hatch up behind him.

Force recon was working squad-size ten-day patrols around the DMZ. It was nerve-racking, isolated work, and the men were always glad to see the helicopters come for them. A HU1E gun ship flew cover as the larger helicopter touched down in the middle of a protective circle of recon Marines which broke off immediately as the men ran up the rear ramp into the helicopter. The aircraft took off fast and without incident.

A sergeant with a five-day beard insisted on shaking hands with the two crewmen before settling down on the red-webbing seat. Most of the others began falling asleep immediately. The gunner glanced at them, then back out over his machine gun. He was in time to see the series of quick flashes on the ground.

There was a vibrating bang towards the rear of the helicopter as something hit. The recon men snapped awake, except for the sergeant, who was smiling in his sleep. The gunner felt them staring at him as he swung the barrel around and returned fire. His tracers curved lazily towards the flashes, bracketing them. He heard Sam open up at a target on his side and then the ground fire stopped abruptly. The HU1E dived below them, strafing, and then firing a rocket.

Sam motioned for a recon-man to stand by his gun, and then ran to the rear. The engine sounded strong and steady. "Nice shooting," said DeLeon's voice in his helmet. "Any damage or casualties back there?"

"Nossir," Sam answered. "Nobody hurt. There's a little hole port-side, but nothin' vital I can see. Engine seems fine." He ran back to his gun mount, nodding thanks to the recon-man.

Minutes later, they were at Dong Ha. They dropped off the recon squad and took off for home. The gunner felt better. His strange mood had disappeared with the fine feeling of competence from the shooting.

He relaxed, feeling sleepy, but methodically scanning the country below. He divided the area passing beneath him into segments, then, beginning at the front of the helicopter, scanned each segment in turn. He was almost unaware of what he was doing, the routine of watching reducing everything to the comfort of technique. The helicopter droned and he was a functioning part of the drone.

He shifted his sight to the front of the helicopter, and his complacency left him. Cauliflower trees and a village coming up fast.

He saw it like that: the helicopter suspended in space and the village attached to some moving assembly-line strip of ground that was drawing it towards the aircraft. For adjustment. It didn't surprise him when he saw a string of green tracers flash up from a clump of trees.

"Gunner, didn't you see the fire," asked DeLeon's voice in his helmet. He didn't answer. They were drawing out of range. I'm going around, the voice said. Let's take care of those people. He looked at the umbilical cord connecting him to the cockpit. The cord was attaching him heavily to DeLeon, as if one of the hairs on the pilot's face had elongated, swelled, grown fleshy. The hollow sick feeling returned and welled in him, spilling from his pores and dirtying him. Gunner, the voice in his ears said, you have the first shot. The village drew under him again. There was no firing from below now. Somebody was probably getting hell for opening up on a single helicopter. Getting hell. He pointed the barrel of the machine gun and to the left of the area he wanted to hit. There was nobody in front of the doorway now. His fingers touched the butterfly trigger, a butterfly touch. He hesitated. Sam was watching him.

THE AMERICAN
READER

THE FIRST TIME ĐÀO THỊ CAM SEES AMERICANS THEY
are bathing in a stream about a thousand meters from where she and
two of her girlfriends lie watching through the foliage. The soldiers'
voices don't carry that far, though she can see they are splashing, probably laughing, their skin occasionally flashing like daylight through the
leaves. She wishes she could get closer, but if Ninh, the male section
leader, learns they have even gotten this close, they will all be in trouble.

She wants to see them, these enemies, translated into flesh from
the tattered Steinbecks and Hemingways and Londons she carries in
her rucksack. Her aunt's treasures, given to Cam when she had joined
the Volunteers, gone south to keep open the Trail. For strength, her
aunt had said. And she was a teacher and a good revolutionary, and
the authors were approved for good revolutionaries, yes, but sometimes
after a bombing or strafing, the other girls would look at Cam with
bitter astonishment. The American reader. Sometimes the adjective
edged into a sharp noun. Yet always a wistfulness in their teasing as
well, as if what Cam is holding onto is something they can't name but
feel sliding out of themselves as well, day by day.

She strains now to see the Americans through the screen of leaves.
They are torn apart in her mind and she needs to knit them together
if she is going to knit herself together. They are still Tom Joad, moving

towards a vision of a perfected, kind world, as she, when she remembers, imagines herself doing, moving through the dust of a space she finds unimaginable in the closeness of the jungle—even though they seem now to be trying to turn that jungle, those trees, into that same bowl of dust and emptiness Joad had fled to a greener land. They are Robert Jordan, lying on his stomach, watching the bridge, as she lies on her stomach, watching Jordan's compatriots now, and she is Marie, waiting in the encompassing warmth of his sleeping bag, for the warmth of flesh and connection against the coldness of death. They are a man trying with his hands to build a fire as the circle of howling wolves closes in on him, as her own hands, her fingers, work frantically to prevent the fire blossoming from the guts of the bomb that moments before had howled down from them to her; they are the machines that come to kill her and hers; they are the red flashing of tracers through the jungle canopy, the masked, mirroring face hovering above, the sudden light shivering like panic through the branches. They are a weight in her rucksack, the books that anchor her; they give her paths she can follow along the paths she must follow; they give her the courage to face themselves. They are these naked boys in a jungle pond, though they are too far away to really see anything, her friend complains in a whisper, and the other two girls giggle. They are too far away to see anything, she thinks, because they are ghosts, they are lines in a book, they are too many contradictions to be real, to be flesh, to be naked.

• • •

They are flying over Helicopter Valley, with its cupped wreckage, when DeLeon's scream pierces the gunner's ears, a sound so filled with terror and despair that, filtered through earphone static, he hears it as a wail spiraling up from the broken aircraft below them. The helicopter jerks, up and then down. He traverses the ground with the barrel of the machine gun. He sees no tracers, has heard nothing hit the plane. He risks a glance over at the two prisoners they'd picked up at LZ Crow, drags the flashed afterimage of them quickly back to his stare out of the port. The recon Marine sitting across from them hadn't moved. His M-14 on his lap, his finger on the trigger. The two in olive-green North Vietnamese Army uniforms tattered, muddy and bloody, but not faded. New guys. Sitting motionless also, the base of a triangle, the recon Marine the apex, their eyes dulled, heads leaning towards each other, side by side, as if still fastened together by the wire the Nungs who had captured them had punctured through their cheeks. The Marine—he was a staff sergeant—had cursed and pulled it out when they'd been handed over, the two North Vietnamese jerking like fish as he did it. The holes in their cheeks scabbed over now, but still bleeding red slick snail trails down their swollen cheeks. Tears from strange eyes. The staff sergeant's eyes dulled also, his head tilting in fatigue.

The noise from the cockpit—curses, scuffles—hasn't abated. Sam keys his mike: "Sir, what's happening?"

"A fucking snake," the co-pilot, Anderson says, his voice more exasperated than fearful.

A *snake*, he says again, indignantly, and the word, the hot, poisonous sibilance of it, opens into Everything. Into the jagged carpet of smashed helicopters below them. Into the impossible, malevolent, steam bath of tangled, vine-strangled, insect-crawling, breezeless, lightless at midday, hundred-foot-tall triple-canopy jungle they were over again now. Into the men they'd set down in it and taken out, sucked dry like insects caught in a web. Into clouds of hot, red laterite dust sucked into engines at takeoff, the nerve-racking dance of hands and feet on collective and cyclic and pedals, a manic weave on the loom of the very centrifugal force that wants to tear the thousands of pieces of machinery to pieces; into landing too hot and too heavy and downwind on slopes picketed with trees, the heavy wet air pushing down the helicopter loaded with its weight of flesh and equipment; all the deadly specific numbers: thirteen grunts times eighty pounds each of steel helmets, M-14s, web belts hung with grenades and loaded magazines and full canteens and entrenching tools and machetes and flak jackets and field packs, not to mention the M-60 machine guns or mortars the weapons platoons carried, not to mention the 150 to 200 pound eighteen to twenty-year-old bodies carrying all of it, not to mention the helicopter's own machine guns and ammunition and flak-jacketed crew and 2,200 pounds of fuel, all optimal conditions needed to suck the lift right from under blades, to wind down, as if it were the clock of your life, the RPM that kept you in the air; to stop rotor blades like a hand stuck into a fan, to feel yourself a gracefully floating dandelion suddenly puffed on from above by a malevolent hot-breathed giant, to be slammed into the terrain below, into other helicopters, into screaming men and suddenly liberated fifty-foot-long blades slicing through air foliage torsos necks heads arms and later you come down and see someone still sitting behind a log as if taking a break and you pick up what turns out to be only the top half of a sergeant, lighter that way, and yes, a clean-cut boy, you think. It's all there, in those words, in the utterly appropriate hissed curse of them: the 12.7 mm North Vietnamese antiaircraft guns and B-40 rockets and quad-fifty machine guns that send orange and green fireballs streaking past the ports, and the ship you'd watched go down yesterday, thick black smoke streaming from the fuel line the incendiary round had hit, smashing into the ridge, rolling on its back, bursting into flames, a random pyre auto-rotating frantically as if to blow out its own flames before twisting over, breaking its rotored back on the ground, the sheet of flame moving through the compartment, the two men jumping out of the back, one too high, to his death; the other too low, the flaming mass falling on top of him, and the rest all gone by then, burning bright in that forest of eternal night. And, if that wasn't enough, there were the prisoners dragged to the rear ramp like fish flopping on a wire, and the grenade your allies from the Army of the Republic of Vietnam Itself had left wedged under a red-webbed seat, and the wounded and dead you'd scooped out of the black meat-grinding, fire-seared night. And if, just in case, by any chance, as Vietnam would have it, to top it all, if that wasn't enough, then you could still have a fucking snake in your cockpit.

• • •

She looks at her friends, Sương and Thu Hà, their faces shaded under the floppy green jungle hats, but scratched, smudged, hollow-cheeked with hunger, gums bleeding, teeth loose. If she could see their bodies under the clothes that hung like rags on them, she would see ribs pushing against paper-thin flesh over stomachs bloated with hunger, nets of scars and scratches, insect bites and scabies. They are all like that. She understands what bodies are. She understands the hungers, shares them; they are all young, girls and boys, and they breathe and sleep with death as if they are old, and they want their lives, and they all understand a life can be folded like an endless cloth into ten minutes that you can slowly draw back out and touch and savor all the rest of your life, however long it goes on from that moment. When bodies are laid out on the broken earth they look like part of it. People go south dressed and they come back dead, and that direction itself has come to mean death, and she helps bury them, the dead, though sometimes they are wounded and sometimes she holds them, the way the woman in Steinbeck held the starving man against her breast and gave him suck, and they call her mother, though she's younger than them, and she remembers how, in her village, before she'd gone south, the bombs had struck before the time people knew they needed to build shelters and she'd come back from the school outing to see the bodies huddled under the trees, mothers and fathers with children clutched and melted to their chests. And sometimes they are the other girls or boys from her unit, and often the bombs blast the clothing from their bodies so they go into their deaths as they had come into their births and she had at first, more than death itself, feared that exposure. But she is seventeen now and she knows that death makes everyone sexless. In a line of bodies, what caught your eye was how little difference there was, how easily it could be erased. Her thoughts are scrambled, confused, and mixed now with the dim white figures seen through the screen of leaves, the ghosts that would kill her.

• • •

"Where, sir?" the gunner says nervously, keying his mike. He is hearing curses, scrambling noises through the earphones. "Shit," DeLeon says, his voice high-pitched.

"No joy, no joy," Anderson says. "No visual contact."

"It went behind the instrument panel!"

"Are you sure?" Anderson's voice. "I think it's a fucking viper."

I'm de vindow viper. Punch line of an old joke. The gunner looks down nervously at his feet. Sweat rolls down his neck, under the collar of his flight suit, crawls down his back; he wants to turn, search, raise his legs, dance like a mad bagpiper. He feels his skin contracting under the leg of his flight suit, his muscles spasming up to his thighs. Snake crawl. *I'm de bamboo viper.* He thinks of it sliding behind the HAC and co-pilot, through the hatch, under the web seats, or along the wiring over his head. Hears, suddenly, the voice of the flight commander, Colonel Watson in his ICS, asking them what the problem is.

The helicopter had reared out of formation—they are flying in a division, four helicopters—when DeLeon let go of the collective. The pilot had pulled out his Ka-Bar knife and hacked at the snake, which had dropped heavily to the deck, shot like an arrow between Anderson's rubber foot pedals into the tangle of wires behind the instrument panel. Straightened up and slithered off, the gunner hears DeLeon say, with the near-hysterical hilarity which means, the gunner knows, that the incident has already become a war story, will be told everywhere, was humming through the ether even now.

But the snake is still in the aircraft, had not yet crawled into the safety of story. For all he knows it is still coiled around wires behind the panels, cunning, camouflaging itself as part of the technology, using the machinery of the enemy against the enemy. Low crawling, naked and slick, a sapper coming through the wire. Touched my elbow like a kiss, slid along the aluminum ledge under the window, he hears DeLeon say to Anderson. *I'm the vindow viper.* Green-brown in complexion, maybe three foot tall, skinny as a pencil, DeLeon says. He's talking to them now. Fanged and dangerous. Find the fucker. Take no prisoners.

"A fucking snake," Anderson says, and the gunner can feel it, sense the snake, moving under the deck plates, sneaking through the avionics. Staying just ahead of or just behind them. He glances down, involuntarily. Something to the left of his left foot. Green and brown. He looks at the staff sergeant. He still hasn't moved, and neither have the prisoners. They're each other's stories too, but they don't know the end yet. The gunner slowly picks up the M-1 carbine he'd bought for ten dollars from an ARVN as a back-up weapon. Stops. What the hell is he going to do, shoot it through the deck? He carefully leans the carbine against the ammo catcher, slides out his Ka-bar knife. It hasn't moved. Playing dead, he thinks. *I'm the vindow viper and I've come to vipe your vindow.* He stares. He should be looking out of his port. It is getting rapidly dark. But the enemy is here. It's too still. Too . . . dull. Inanimate. It can't be a snake. He slowly advances the point of the knife, pushes down swiftly. Like a snake striking. The object is solid. Un-snake-like. He slowly squats, thinking *grenade*. No. A small book. He picks it up, impaled, pulls it off the blade, realizing, too late, it may be a booby-trap anyway. No. It doesn't explode. There's a black and white picture of a girl inside, a young couple in front of an iron gate fashioned into a circle of Chinese ideograms. But the writing on the stained pages, cribbed and lined through and smudged and blurring in the waning light, is Vietnamese writing, regular letters tortured top and bottom with little barbed wire spikes. The written lines broken, as if poetry. Probably belonged to one of the prisoners. He should give it to the sergeant. Snake's diary, he thinks. Viper story. The two prisoners and the sergeant are still staring at each other, motionless as a diorama, as if all three have been wired together. The small book burns his hand, through his flight glove, as if it has dripped venom on him. He straightens up, quickly tosses it out of his port. Follows it with his machine gun barrel, twisting and fluttering in the air, white pages winging against dark sky, the photos flying out like released spirits.

• • •

It is growing dark, and is darker yet under the thick-knit branches can-opied over the creek where she bathes. It is the same pool, a widening of the creek really, where the Americans had bathed. Cam can hardly see the bank. Knows she can't be seen. Suddenly the noise of rotors beats down on top of the leaves like fists beating on a door, and she freezes until it fades off, leaving only its echoes and then the memory of its echoes. She thinks, taking herself away from it, how she will make all this into story, mix has-been with could-be; fold the story over her-self like a camouflage shelter as the bombs fall closer. This urgency to immerse herself in the same water, she thinks, to take the mystery of them into her skin, she thinks, and her mind tries to flee the thought, but she has trained herself to clutch at those fugitives of her being; they were, in the end, the whispers that named her. She has a broken sliver of soap from a bar that Thu Hà had brought back from Hanoi, a luxury, and she soaps herself, and now she hums the tune to an Italian song all of the girls from Hanoi remember and sing. She has dirt under her nails from the Trail, from the dirt they shoveled back into the craters, smoothing them for the trucks going south, and her fingers stink from the gelignite they'd packed around the bomb she had embraced earlier in the day, helped lower into a hole, blown up. She scrubs her hands and her body, at the words she feels written on her back, seeped through her rucksack and into her skin. She is unable to even see her flesh now, feels herself borderless, dissolving into the water, the darkness, the insect hum. The Americans she had seen that day come again to her mind, and she lets them float next to her for a moment, and then lets them go.

• • •

As the book falls, the helicopter formation wheels west, over the moun-tainous jungle of the cordillera. A place filled with snakes. The darkness is not so much beginning to cover it as it is entering it, like an injected liquid, the top of the jungle canopy configuring into ominous, fluid shapes. Leaf people. Anderson's voice is in the gunner's ear again, his words repeated by DeLeon: they want him and Sam to fire into the fleshy mass below. Into the trees. They think Something is down there. No shit. It's the snake's home. The place of snakes. The home of the snake and the land of the viper. He fires down into it. As he does, he sees an artillery barrage begin, over to the west of their flight path, aircraft diving down, as if called by his fire. A hot shell casing falls on his neck, stings like a snake bite. He fires more, his shoulders shaking, hands vibrating, fires at the ghosts moving under the trees, fires at a girl he imagines just as she tries to imagine his face behind the wind and the fire and the noise and the fragmented light. His rounds curve and streak down far from where she crouches, hidden, watching, and the darkling green absorbs them so quickly it is as if they never existed at all.

MORATORIUM

*Mor*a*to*ri*um, n. 1. an authorization to delay payment due*

DEBORAH ASKED, "EVERYTHING ALL RIGHT?"

"Just the early morning broods."

She watched his hands as he soaped them.

"I'm still scared of how you're taking it."

"How am I taking it?"

"Too seriously. Like some momentous, ceremonial occasion. But it's just a party to most of the people. That's why I stopped going."

"I thought you stopped going because of me."

"That's what I mean."

They sat down on the bed, settling back against the pillow. She put her head on his chest.

In our Operations tent, he said, there was this gunny sergeant; he kept a framed photograph on his desk. Not the wife and kids, but this picture from the *New York Times*, a shot of one of the first demonstrations. He'd circled one marcher's head with a grease pencil he used on the flight status board to write in the names of the crews going on missions. Above the guy's head he wrote, "Traitor—to be killed." The circle was real thick and dark, and you could see he'd pressed down very hard with rage because of the smudge where the tip of the pencil had broken off.

"Nobody's going to draw a halo around your head," Deborah said.

He got off the bed and walked over to the closet. The night before, he'd hung up his jungle shirt and some jeans and hooked the hanger over the door, ready as if he were going on an early morning flight, a mission. He'd pinned his silver aircrew wings to the shirt. The gunny, he remembered suddenly, was the kind of NCO who would write people up for chickenshit, stateside offenses like being out of uniform, as if he felt he had a mission to maintain standards, standards that didn't apply in the circumstances of the war.

He put on the shirt, running his fingertips over the metal wings. A knock startled him. He waited until Deborah had pulled on a long shirt and then he opened the door.

Barry was wearing a khaki shirt with his ribbons and Combat Infantry Badge on it. He grinned: their choice of clothing hadn't been planned.

"Green side out," he said. "How you feeling?"

"Traitor—to be killed."

"There it is."

They made a pit stop at Maryland House. The two men had a smoke while they waited for Deborah and Barry's girl Phyllis to get out of the restroom. He had another while Barry pumped the gas. A silver-gray Plymouth pulled up next to them. In the passenger seat was a blonde woman with a beehive hairdo. She glanced at him, then patted her hair, as if his gaze had made her conscious of it. The driver was wearing a khaki uniform, Army Class A's, like Barry's, a colored rectangle of ribbons on his chest. The woman tilted the mirror again and a rhomboid of light projected over the face of the soldier inside. The face looked vaguely accusing and pissed off. He'd been holding a kind of tension, he realized, since the day before, since he'd decided to go to the demonstration. Now something in the angle of light, in the blurred features of the face, allowed that tension to relax in a kind of internal collapse into the face of Jim Hardesty.

Hardesty was a boy who had died in his place, flying gunner on a routine resupply mission to Hill 327 during what was to have been the last week of the war for both of them. The squadron was rotating to

Okinawa to get new helicopters; it had lost five aircraft and the remain-
ing ships were in bad shape after four solid months of operations along
the DMZ. He and Jim Hardesty were in the last increment to leave. On
nearly the last day he had drawn flight duty, but Hardesty had asked
if he could take it instead. He couldn't even remember the reason for
it, he didn't know Hardesty that well; they weren't really friends, just
military acquaintances. Maybe Hardesty figured he'd be called to fly
the next day anyway and wanted to get it over with; maybe he needed
a mission for an air medal. There were enough stories of people killed
in the last days of their tours. Outside the war, you told stories like that
to prevent them from happening to you. But, in the war, telling them
was more like calling something to life. If Hardesty wanted to take his
place, that was fine with him. They'd gone to the operations sergeant,
the one with the photograph on his desk, and made the switch. That
night the helicopter in which he would have flown gunner went on a
standard resupply flight to a company of grunts. It was on approach
when it came under fire, and a single bullet hit the helicopter and pene-
trated it and Hardesty's body, going through the gunner's seat where he
would have been sitting, entering below the bottom edge of Hardesty's
flak jacket instead of his, traveling perpendicularly through Hardesty's
body instead of his.

Now he stood alive in a gas station in Maryland watching the face
of a soldier watching him from behind a windshield.

He wondered if the request to switch had been a last-minute effort
on Hardesty's part to deal with some perceived internal weakness while
he still had the chance. There were people who came to the war for that.
Perhaps many people. He remembered how scared Hardesty had been.
In the old aviator's canard, he wasn't afraid of flying, only of coming
down. The country itself filled Hardesty with terror; it was so unlike
the flat Kansas plains he came from. It pulsed with the over-lush greens
of an evil Oz. The fragmented mirrors of its paddies held images of broken helicopters in their depths. Its jagged, broody cordilleras and secre-
tive triple-canopied jungle randomly and maliciously spat fire upwards.

The helicopters would only touch the land briefly to release men onto it, then touch briefly again soon after to pick up the bodies of the same men, torn as if they had been gnawed by the country. What happened in the time between was unknown to the helicopter crews. Hardesty had told him how his finger had started to tremble on the trigger even in cold LZs as if on some hair trigger inside himself that was wearing closer and closer to the sear. He'd understood Hardesty; he was worn in the same places; he sat in the same seat; he knew the feeling of helplessness. On missions, the gunner was an impotent spectator except when shooting his gun. His helicopter had flown cover on one insert when Hardesty's helicopter had let off a squad of grunts and the crews had watched in horror, not frozen, but hovering, darting, hosing the tree line with fire, but all of it useless as the grunts ran in fire-team rushes toward that tree line, falling, one fire team after another cut down, and not one hesitating, just working, moving professionally toward the trees that were killing them; one man after another zigging and zagging and falling as if it were some well-rehearsed, tactically planned process they were all following to get killed quickly. Then on Hardesty's next flight, his helicopter developed a hydraulic leak and had to autorotate down to a hard landing in a paddy, the ship spinning, the land sucking him down to itself. A clearly pregnant woman squatted among the rice shoots, watching him come into her life. She'd frozen, war-wise, knowing that the helicopters shot anyone who ran, not knowing that Hardesty was in this one. That night he'd joked about getting two gooks with one round. Later the crew chief cast doubts on Hardesty's story, saying the gunner was too shaky to hit anything. But the phrase became a standard with the air crews, a measure of shooting proficiency. A joke.

The face behind the windshield mouthed silently at him. He saw the woman put a hand on the soldier's shoulder, as if restraining him.

The memories were coming faster, some compressed spring he'd lived with so long its tightness had become normal suddenly released in his mind. He remembered how he'd flown back to Travis Air Force Base in San Francisco on the same C-130 with about twenty other men from his squadron whose tours had finished while they were on Okinawa. It was the nearest thing the war had to the traditional coming back as a unit: the random mathematics of their time in country giving them an accidental parade, even if it only consisted of being herded up the ramp of the cargo plane together. For the first time they wore the khaki Class A uniforms they hadn't seen for over a year, whitened crease lines on them where the cloth had been folded in their stored sea-bags, new ribbons and silver combat aircrew wings bright on their chests. Perhaps noticing the wings, some of the Air Force crew brought them coffee; they had wings too; they were all birdmen, brothers of the air. How was it, the airmen had asked, and the Marines told them sea stories, air stories, shot down stories, shoot up the village stories, toss the prisoners stories. He told how Hardesty had gotten two gooks with one round. But the airmen didn't laugh. They didn't get the joke. They looked at the Marines, at the wings on their chests, strangely. Then the Marines fell silent, too. They blinked as if awakening from a dream in which the laws and customs of the world had been suspended. He could feel a silence folding around them and he knew that they, he, wouldn't talk about the war anymore, or if they did, they'd try to fit it into more expected and acceptable references. That nobody would get the joke.

"What are you men doing?"

He saw that the soldier had gotten out of the Plymouth. Focusing back, he realized that he hadn't even noticed the process; it played in his mind like a memory behind the memories of that flight home and Hardesty: the car door opening, the frowning face, the woman tugging the soldier's arm, trying to pull him back. There were silver first lieutenant's bars on the man's collar. His eyes went automatically to the ribbons. The yellow and red Vietnam service ribbon was there, but there were no CIB, no wings, no purple heart, only the been-there ribbons.

"I said what are you men doing?" The lieutenant frowned at them.

"You men?" Barry said, squinting at him.

The lieutenant's face went red. "Let me see your IDs."

Barry laughed. "Look, L.T., we're not in the service anymore."

"Then you have no right to be wearing those uniforms. There's a law against impersonating a soldier." He glared at them. "I know where you're going. You're both disgraces. I want your names—both of you."

Barry looked, startled, at the lieutenant, then began laughing. "You want to write me up," he said in wonder. The lieutenant stared at him, still frowning. "You want to write me up now." He laughed more. "Hey, lieutenant, where the fuck were you?" Out of the corner of his eye, he saw Phyllis and Deborah coming back from the ladies' room. "Why don't you just di-di the fuck out of here," he said. "You understand that term, lieutenant? Or you just impersonating a dickhead?"

He saw Barry pull the nozzle out of the gas tank and screw on the cap, his shoulders stiff and high, his face tight. Barry spun around, arcing the gas nozzle close to the lieutenant's face. Some gas globbed from the end and the lieutenant stepped back slightly. Barry nodded and poked the nozzle forward, closer, and the lieutenant backed up. Gas dribbled onto his spit shine. Barry held his lit cigarette in his other hand, between thumb and forefinger. He flicked it. "Ever see a gook flambé, L.T., a crispy critter?" he asked. "Ever write one up? No? Where were you when that was going down? Like the man asked— where the fuck were you? Some office? Pointing your pointer at some map overlay, some grid I was on? Want a ciggie? Souvenir you Salem? Want a light? No? Then like my friend said, you better di-di. Don't let your alligator mouth overload your lizard ass and all that other kind of Vietnam talk."

The lieutenant stared at him. "You men will hear about this, I promise you. I have your license number."

The woman in the Plymouth stuck her head out of the window. "Leave them alone, Martin. We're late."

"You're late, Martin," he said, coming up next to Barry. "Move on, lieutenant pogue. You got my number—give me a call sometime."

The lieutenant left. He turned around. Deborah and Phyllis were staring at him and Barry in the same way Deborah had stared at his hands that morning.

The movement of the march trembled between the buildings. He felt an answering shudder in his chest. He couldn't see either end of the column. On the car radio they'd heard there were half a million people in the streets of Washington. The announcer had commented that this was the equivalent of the number of troops still in Vietnam. Similar numbers were reported from New York, San Francisco, Chicago.

He tried to hang onto a feeling of purposefulness in being part of the movement of so many people. But instead he found himself settling into the dullness he always assumed when marching in a column, an interior blankness that he moved in until he got where he was going. The people around him were linking arms, smiling at each other, chanting for peace now. He lip-synched the words, feeling self-conscious. Deborah had been pushed a little ways from him, and a woman hooked her arm with his and grinned at him. Her other arm was linked with a priest's. The priest smiled at him too. He saw the priest's gaze brush the wings on his chest, the man catching his eye, nodding in approval. Brothers of the air. He brought his hand up, covered the insignia. He had the wings, he needed the halo. I'm out of uniform, priest. Write me up. The chanting grew louder. Phyllis, Barry's arm draped over her shoulder, looked around at him. She was smiling, too. I can't hear you, she mouthed. All of a sudden he was back in boot camp. Get back and do it again. Get it right this time. I can't hear you. All the people around him were chanting and grinning as if they knew something about it, moving their signs and banners up and down in a cadence. They didn't know, but they'd been told. I can't hear you! he yelled. He thought how they would look without the noise coming from their mouths, the way he would turn down the sound on the TV and watch the grotesque panto-mimes of the news announcers, their inane smiles encompassing images of corpses and shooting men and burning hootches. When he'd first gotten back, before he met Deborah, he'd rented a small room and spent hours watching TV, as if he could plug himself back into the country, get back on some wavelength he was missing. On the screen, little gray figures ran across paddies, fell, rose; he was one of them, escaped right out of the box, loose in the streets. Out of uniform. Impersonating a human being. "PEACE NOW!" he yelled, and laughed. The woman and the priest laughed too, but he laughed louder, until they looked at him uneasily. He could get the two of them with one round. They were all bunched up with someplace to go. He couldn't see Deborah. Suddenly a truck pulled in front of him from a side street, breaking into the crowd. It was draped with VC and North Vietnamese flags and there was a rock band on its bed, playing very hard, the marching band for this parade. The music jerked the crowd. He could see one of the player's faces very clearly. It was pale and pimpled, and the boy's eyes were blank as if all his emotions had been poured into the blurred motion of his fingers on the guitar strings. The boy had made a VC flag into a vest, was bare-chested under it, his upper body white and skinny. He stared at the boy's face. He wanted to break it with his fist, knead expressions into it, give it to Jim Hardesty. But the face stayed blank. His feelings didn't particularly move it.

"Hey, man," he yelled at the boy. "Hey, you're out of uniform." The boy cupped one hand behind his ear and smiled helplessly. He didn't get the joke.

He looked away from the boy, searching for Deborah; she'd been squeezed a little further forward. He spotted Barry and Phyllis near her. They were looking up at the spectators in the windows of government office buildings, searching for anyone cheering them from behind the walls of legitimate authority. Some of the windows had jungly green plants behind them, as if screening another world that hid behind the facade of the building. Faces peered at him in silent disapproval. They had his number. The lieutenant's face mouthed angrily at him from behind the glass. It blurred and disappeared.

Move on, lieutenant pogue.

He'd stopped to look up at the windows, letting the crowd break around him. When he looked back down, he couldn't see Deborah anywhere. He felt a sense of trapped panic. He began shoving through the marchers. The crowd was a pressure at his temples. He pushed through, feeling bodies like vines and roots, holding his passage for an instant, then giving way and slipping past him. He grasped with his hands in a swimming motion, taking people by the shoulders and parting them out of his way. They glared at him, but said nothing until he was past; then they'd start chanting again as if he'd never touched them. "Over here!" he heard Deborah yell. She was next to the priest. He made a final thrust and broke through, reaching out blindly, connecting with the priest's arm. He gripped it. All those personnel wishing halos will assemble to the right and rear of the duty priest. Semper fi, sky pilot, you got yours, how'm I doing? The priest was staring at him. He released his arm.

You're late, sky pilot, he thought. Move on. Don't let your alligator intentions overload your lizard dimensions.

They were moving now through a gap in a row of parked school buses and into the Mall area. As the column broke and spread into the clearing, he could see for the first time the vastness of the crowd. It filled the center of the city, the white tower of the monument rising from its center. "Half a million people," Deborah said into his ear, half a million was his number and he could see it unabstract, solidly filling space. He could see with his eyes what half a million was. He felt utterly outside them, on the other side of a hard, transparent screen. The half million were laughing and dancing and he tried to think about Jim Hardesty who'd died in his place and the woman and the future Hardesty had killed from his place and in their name, these people around him who wouldn't look at him, and he looked at them and he could see how they would be dead, all dead and lying on the grass, silent and spilling into the earth. I can't hear you, he thought. He sat down where he was. He was waiting for something inside himself and when it finally came he began crying. It came in waves so hard he felt they had to move out of him, ripple through the hugeness of the crowd. But when he looked up, he only saw a woman staring as if surprised at what he was doing. He couldn't stop it. There was no release in it. Deborah put a hand on his shoulder. He bowed his head back down, pressing his face against the cloth of his shirt, and the noise faded again. It was as if he were alone in the cradle of his arms.

THE SERPENT

THE RONDEZVOUS BAR AND LOUNGE SITS OFF ONE OF the main side roads in the county. If not for that misspelled sign in front of the gravel parking lot, the permanently sputtering and fly speckled neon Budweiser advertisement, and the Happy Hour sign behind the dirt-filmed glass of the window, it could be taken for the house of a heartbroken widower who no longer gave a damn: loose boards, green paint peeling off loose boards, a porch shaded by a sagging tin overhang, the roof shingles winged up here and there or missing in patches, with the underlying creosote sheets showing through like wounds. The sign always bothered me when I drove by the place, as if the misspelled French would confirm some redneck stereotype of the county to visitors. Once I pulled in, had a beer, and mentioned the mistake in the spelling to the owner, Tom Delaney. Delaney, a three-hundred-pound man with a shaved head, Fu Manchu mustache, prison tattoos and cigarette burn scars on hairy arms, had lowered his head, looked at me and growled, "What are you, a Democrat?"

He gave me the same look as I came in now. He was wearing a black Harley-Davidson t-shirt, sagging black jeans, and scuffed engineer boots. He wiped the bar counter with a rag that looked like it could have been used to wipe grease from his motorcycle, if he had had one. He didn't. Some of the tattoos that had been on his arms were gone also, replaced by the red burn and pucker of laser scars, defoliated patches in the pelt that covered his arms. The tattoos had included the shamrock symbols of the Aryan Brotherhood, but as it turned out, he'd never been in prison or owned a motorcycle. In fact, he drove a Subaru wagon and had bought the bar, apparently fulfilling the shape of some lifelong dream, after he'd sold an arts and crafts supply store his family had owned in PG County. When I'd gotten his background information from our sheriff, Russell Hallam, I'd felt disappointed: it turned out both he and the bar were concepts themselves, like the '50s-style diners I'd see in Bethesda or Tysons Corner or Annapolis, as if nothing of my time could be anything but shadows on the cave wall, as if it all had to legitimize itself through older models. Delaney's tattoos had gone after some actual Aryan brothers had seen them and had given him a choice between erasure and amputation.

As far as I knew, though, none of the other clientele saw the bar or Delaney as anything more than they purported to be. I'd never told anyone what Hallam had told me about Delaney, and as long as the Brotherhood didn't come around, he was a man content in his reinvention, at it for so long that he'd become it.

As soon as my eyes adjusted to the darkness, I spotted Joleen Baird, sitting in a booth near the toilet, a glass and a nearly empty pitcher of draft beer in front of her, her finger pushing thin wakes out of the net of foam on the scarred tabletop. She was the only customer, which, it being ten in the morning, was not surprising, though not always the case. She turned to me, and I saw her in the light of the Coors neon waterfall near the mirror. She looked lacquered. I don't mean drunk. It was the word that came into my mind as I stared at her. As if someone had poured a gallon of lacquer over her head that had stiffened and sheened her. Her blonde hair sat like a helmet on her head, and her face, bright red lipstick, penciled eyebrows, artificial lashes, looked as if a wax death mask had been fastened to it. Like the bar and Delaney, she'd become a painting of herself. Thinking that, I remembered how in middle school I'd tried to earnestly explain to her the correct spelling of her name, some early marker, I suppose, of my journalistic predisposition. It should be J-o-l-e-n-e, I told her. Later, I found out that the spelling she used came from her mother, Lurleen, who either didn't know the right spelling, didn't care, or wanted to tag their names together. At the time though—we were on a school field trip—she didn't explain, just threw me off the dock where we were sitting, into Milburn Creek.

I ordered another pitcher from Delaney. As I reached for it, he seized my wrist.

"You all be gentle now," he growled.

I twisted away, and then we both looked down at the bar, as if the beer spills and beaded scrawls of liquid on it were runic puzzles.

"No problem, Tom," I said.

I took the pitcher and a glass and went over to the booth.

"Have a seat, hon," she said. She wasn't slurring her words. Her eyes looked as dead as the rest of her face. Her lips barely moved as she spoke. It was like I was interviewing an oracle. In high school Joleen had always seemed older than her age, one of those girls wise with some sardonic knowledge she'd inherited from a long line of women who were never disappointed because they never had any expectations. One day her mother had burst into our classroom to cuss out her teacher and drag Joleen out of school: a foul-mouthed, obese woman with blotched skin, dressed in a halter top that lifted cleavage that looked like flabby buttocks, too-tight jean shorts bulged with her actual behind, her pasty and stubbled legs bruised with needle scars. Lurleen had brought along her then-boyfriend, a black man half her size and wearing a lime green suit, yellow shirt with flared collar, and pointed, patent-leather shoes. Such couples weren't unusual in the county, and I'd never thought much about it before. But unable to bear looking at Joleen, who'd sat two rows across from me, wearing an expression of the most abject humiliation I'd ever seen on a human face, I'd concentrated on him instead. He was silent, just nodding now and then at his woman's string of obscenities at Mrs. Colby, who, apparently, had questioned some bruises she had seen on Joleen's face. In spite of his clothes, he'd not been a bad-looking guy, and it made me wonder about the depth of racial wounds and insecurity that would make Lurleen Elliott seem a trophy to him.

Joleen didn't go back to school after that day, and I hadn't seen her again until I saw copy and a photo for her wedding announcement in my paper, the *Reporter*. She had not taken on her mother's obesity; in fact looked too thin, meth or crack thin, I'd thought, but her eyes were shining in the photo. Her fiancé, Jonathan Baird, was a black man also, and when I'd first heard that, I thought of her mother and wondered if Joleen had inherited her racism, for I'd come to think that was the other side of her mother's string of relationships with certain kinds of black men; either cashing in on the overdrawn account of her skin and its privileges, or punishing herself for being herself by becoming a punch-board payback for 400 years of bad times. But Baird was not a dealer or thief; he was the pastor of The Holy Church of the Redeeming Christ, a Baptist, storefront operation. To my surprise, Joleen invited me to the wedding—one of a group of people she had known in high school from social circles that tended to look down at her own as trailer trash, and who, I figured out later, had all been in the classroom that day. She'd needed, I realized, to show us this, as if to replace the scene she assumed burned in our memories as it must have in hers. I came—I was only one of three who did—and I'd found I liked Baird; a tall, slender man with bright, intelligent eyes and a small, arrow-shaped head that seemed incongruous with his deep, Baptist preacher voice. He owned a kind of trembly gentleness with Joleen, as if she was a blessing to his life he was afraid to dissolve with a harsh word or action. She had been the same way with him, at one point in the ceremony, presided over by his sister—also a minister—reaching over and touching his lips with a kind of grateful wonder that wrenched my heart.

"He saved me," she said to me now. She raised her eyes, the mask of her face, and I understood that what she meant was that she was now lost. Whatever she had been was scraped out to her shell.

"Can you tell me about him?"

"Sure I can, honey. But not so's you all will know him. That's the bitch, ain't it, Hunter. You get people looking at you like you're shit, telling you you're shit every day your life; you get a fat bag of hate and spite for a mama, look at you like you something she meant to flush down the toilet, and then you get a miracle. This sweet-touching man who tells you he sees what's shining in you and from you. Shakes when he touches you, each time, like you're a gift he's unwrapping, and every time it's a surprise and a delight to him. Yeah, I know," she reached out and patted my forearm, "you want me to tell you the war. Tell you how it went into his veins like poison. But I gotta tell you, you all got to understand about the sweetness of this man. He talked Jesus and I didn't give a shit about no Jesus, but when I saw my Jonathan, I believed, because I could see Jesus in him, like a shining gentleness. I believed."

"Did you talk to him, when he was over there."

She nodded, pantomimed putting a phone to her ear. "Yeah, sure. Telephone, sometimes. Computer more often. It's so weird, honey, you know he's seeing Lord knows what and you're talking about the broken hot water heater, and the church supper and then he starts talking like I'm not even there, like he's talking to Jesus himself and I'm not more than that telephone, that modem, and he's saying that he's supped with horror. That's the words he uses, that he's supped with horror. What you say to someone, they tell you that? Hey, darlin', I had to have the septic drained and I maxed out the Visa? I mean, they don't make him no chaplain, like he should be, right. But the others, they all pour it into his ears, all their shit and meanness and being scared, cause it don't matter, he's a minister a God and they know it. So they pour it all in."

"Was there any particular stories you remember?"

She laughed. It was a terrible laugh and there was no light in her eyes when she looked at me.

"You want to sup with horror, Hunter?" She picked up her glass, turned it, so the dull red light of the bar gleamed in it. "You want to have a beer with horror? That why you're here?"

"I want to tell his story, Joleen."

"Well, ain't you something. Ain't you something that likes sittin' on the barn roof waiting to see what some dead meat it can pluck and chew. Some road kill on the asphalt."

"Is that what you think?"

She looked away, and then looked back at me and sighed. "No, man. No, you got a good heart, I know that. Know that since you was this gawky thing looked at me like it was your heart breaking stead of mine, my fat bitch of a mother comes to class. I could of killed you that day." A slight smile twitched her lips. "You all want his story, tell the world, all that? Thing is, Hunter, was he didn't have no story. He was what he was here. He listened, Hunter. That's what he did. That's what he did as a preacher. He could shout out with the best, but he could be still and safe too, Hunter. He didn't have no story. He took in everybody else's story. Kid who saw his friends all in pieces around him and tried to stick them back together. Guy who ran over a little girl cause she stood in the road. Guy who saw his own mother and father's faces in the faces of the Iraq family they lined up against the wall, man pissing himself. You heard the stories, honey. He was what he called a receptacle. Know what that means? It's a garbage can. They kept throwing the stories in and he kept trying to bring Jesus out for them, but after a while, he couldn't find him. After a while, he knew he had to sup with horror himself."

"What does that mean?"

"You tell me. You think those words mine?"

"He did something," I said. Not a question.

She filled her glass from the pitcher, drank it down. Laughed.

"Went down to the crossroads, you know those words? Needed to be inside their stories, him, place they lost a Humvee or Bradley, or whatever they call them, and then another, same place, six guys, and he went down there, helped plant a surprise for the hajis or gooks or whatever they call them. So it happened, just like you would figure it would happen you're in a place the worst is always going to happen. Command detonated. Not whatever they call them. Command detonated, his exact words, his finger on the button. Finger of God. Presses the button, smokes the hajigooks who a course turn out to be ma and pa and two little kid gookhajis, coming back from their memaw's or something. Something like that."

She closed her eyes. Her face, which had seemed so stiff, now seemed ready to shatter like the surface of a mirror. "See, Hunter. See, the thing is, Hunter, I did it. I did it to him. Took what I loved most, only gold I found on the surface of the earth, and I turned it into shit."

"I'm sure that's not true, Joleen."

Her eyes blazed. "What the fuck you know about it, you? Don't give me that weak, watery not your fault shit. Who you think you are? My Jonathan, he was the preacher. Not you, asshole."

"I'm sorry."

"That's for sure. I tell you, it's my fault, you fucking listen. I thought that's what you here for."

"I'm listening."

"It was such a damnation stupid thing. Like I thought it would make him feel, maybe not better, but, I don't know, connected, maybe. So we on the computer link, right, and I can like see him, some tan canvas behind him, him blocking out everything else over there, like he's doing it deliberately. You know, shielding me with his body. Those guys take a grenade for their friends? He'd a done that, he was a noble man."

"I know he was."

"You don't know shit. So we're talking, right, and I give him this little bit of information I got from some on-line article or some shit, says that Iraq is where the original Garden of Eden was. And for a long time, he says nothing. Just stares, outta my screen. Then he laughs. It's an awful laugh, Hunter, I can't tell you. Says, 'I am the serpent, baby.' I say, 'my sweet darling, you ain't no such a thing.'" He just looks at me, says, 'Don't make no difference. Once you hear it, once you see it, you know it's there.' Laughing again, shaking his head like it's all clear to him now. Then he cuts the connection."

She put her hand on my forearm again.

"Maybe that's it. Maybe he couldn't shake the devil out. But the thing I keep thinking, maybe it's wrong. I still don't believe he took his own life."

"Why's that?"

"You ever knew a black man hung himself?"

•   •   •

I played the recording to Ashley that evening. Joleen's voice said: "They got too many others willing to do the work." I shut the Marantz. There was more on the tape, but I wasn't sure how I would deal with it, if I would use it in the article at all. What Joleen had described to me went beyond the kind of psychosis I could describe in a newspaper story, and I didn't know if it had to. I kept thinking of Joleen's face when her mother had come into her classroom, the humiliations and wounds of a childhood soothed by the hope that Jonathan Baird had brought into her life.

Ashley held up her hand, as if to physically block Joleen's words. "There's so much God damn pain," she said. "I wish you would just stop now. Turn in this story, and then stop, Hunter."

In bed, we watched a Netflix movie about a Korean ex-convict who falls in love with a girl whose body was twisted with muscular dystrophy; she could only speak in cryptic, bubbly mumbles. It ended sweetly, but was probably not the best film for me to see that night, though later I wished I could have seen its more gentle tendrils in the images that slid into my brain instead. Sleepless, I quietly got out of bed. Ashley stirred, murmured, a bubble of saliva forming on her lips. I went into the kitchen. There was a patter of rain against the window above the sink, the first after a three-week drought though too weak to break it. I opened the window and let the cooling breeze and a mist diffused by the screen wet my face. The whine of the heat pump motor started. I went out to the living room thermostat and turned it off and the noise of the fan shuddered and stopped. I opened the living room windows, heard the rain beating against the surface of the creek, raising and bringing that fecund smell of silt and estuarine salt water, the blood of the earth, to my nostrils. The Marantz recorder lay on the kitchen table like a bomb. I thought of how Joleen described finding her husband;

he'd hung himself in their closet when she went out; his tongue had been blackened, its tip protruding from between his lips. I went to the cabinet, took out a bottle of Jameson's and poured a drink, and then sat in front of the window, the lights off, the occasional flash of lightning illuminating the room, scrambling the shadows into shapes I didn't want to look at. The whiskey burned my mouth, warmed my throat, and I let myself think about the rest of Joleen's interview. For reasons I wasn't certain of myself, I hadn't played it for Ashley.

Joleen had sensed her husband's distance and difference from the beginning. But she hadn't expected him to be untouched. The whole National Guard unit came back together, and all around her families were waving welcome home signs, and then were embracing and kissing their soldiers, laughing. Baird had seen her, and she was grinning enough to split her cheeks, running to him, throwing her arms around him. He embraced her, but his back felt stiff under her hands, a coldness coming off him, as if he'd been sitting next to an air conditioning outlet on the bus, and his lips, when she kissed him, were clenched tight and felt thin and dry under her own, the little lick he darted between her lips more tentative than passionate. She noticed that the other men were hugging each other, giving high fives, shaking hands, saying their farewells, but no one came near her husband. They parted on each side of him, as if he was in a bubble. She thought it strange, since he'd told her how the others would come to him, tell him their stories, and she knew that was true from letters and emails soldiers and their families had sent her, telling her how her Jonathan had been there for them, held their minds in place with the compassion of his eyes and the rock hard grip of his faith, giving them meaning amid the terrible erasures all around them.

They barely spoke on the ride home. He pressed his forehead against the window and looked outside at the passing, familiar scenery, and she thought, good, let it fill him up with green, drive out the terrible tan emptiness which is how she pictured Iraq. In the house, she'd set the table and had prepared his favorite meal, the county dish of ham scored and stuffed with kale and spices, wrapped in cotton and steamed; hot biscuits, collard greens, mashed potatoes and gravy, sun tea in a glass pitcher beaded with condensation. He'd sat rigidly in the chair, his body stretched with tension and swaying slightly, his eyes darting here and there. He took a fork-full of the potatoes, brought it up to his mouth, and licked it slightly, his tongue darting in and out, before putting it in his mouth. Seeing this, Joleen shuddered, and he noticed and looked at her with half-lidded eyes. She felt ashamed.

She stood up, took his hand, and led him to the bedroom. She had anticipated their sexual reunion for months, sustained herself with fantasies. But what she felt now wasn't erotic; it was utilitarian: she would use her body to join him back into their lives. He let himself be led, silently. As she undressed, he sat rigidly on the bed, staring straight ahead without blinking, his body swaying slightly, to and fro. It unnerved her. He let her undress him. Then he began touching her with the tip of his tongue, all over her body. He was not kissing or licking her flesh; all she could think of was the way his tongue had darted out to touch his food. Before, when they'd made love, his skin would always be covered with a thin layer of sweat, and she loved the sharp, salty smell of him, but now his skin was cold and dry. She told herself that it was because his body had become accustomed to the aridity of the desert and had taken it into itself, but when he embraced her and twined himself around her, she couldn't help it, she screamed. He immediately loosened himself from her, and when he looked at her, she saw his eyes were filled with tears, his head swaying. I'm sorry, she started to say, but he slid out of bed, and before she could say anything else, he went to the closet, opened the door and went in, and then closed the door. She lay for a long time, her heart hammering in her chest, trying to block out the sound she heard or thought she heard from behind that white door, air escaping from between pressed lips. She shook her head, got out of bed, crossed the room, and opened the door. He was on the floor, against the back wall, and the skin of his flank, as it caught the light, looked to her like the curve of a coil.

She thought: *what have I brought into my home?*

THE
TWENTY-FIFTH
PLATOON

THAT MAY, WE DROVE ABOUT FORTY CLICKS NORTH OF
Hanoi, past a green and gold patchwork of rice fields, and up into the
mountains. Our small convoy turned off the highway at a dirt road that
wound up to the site: a bowl of rice and corn fields, a red-mudded flat
area, some stone and thatched houses, all held between jungled hills that
stood lushly green against large, jagged limestone peaks. It was raining
and a white mist tendrilled around the black slopes, the green and black
and red melting, a composition in a David Douglas Duncan war photo.

I was working for a joint Vietnamese-Singaporean production
called *Song of the Stork*, as script writer of the scenes that would involve
American soldiers, and now as unofficial advisor for those same scenes.
It was to be the first internationally produced film about the war to
be actually shot in Việt Nam. "Come to Việt Nam this summer and
we'll shoot you in Quảng Trị," the Vietnamese director had told me,
very aware of the resonance in his statement. But since the filming had
begun, another foreign company had been given permission to film
in Việt Nam, a joint Australian-American production of *The Quiet
American*. The film would star Michael Caine, as Greene's cynical
British journalist Fowler, fighting the well-intentioned and hence deadly

American Pyle for the right to exploit Việt Nam (as metaphorically embodied in the usual mysterious and emotionless oriental enigma Phượng) for their own ends. In fact, Phượng was being played by one of our actresses, Hải Yến, who had finished her work on *Stork*. *The Quiet American* dwarfed us, in personnel, in money, in equipment. They had even used some of the sites we had used previously, including the one where we would film today. Looking at it, I saw a ditch lined with rows of sandbags and concertina wire, the red mud around it pocked with holes, some of the foliage blackened. Ammo boxes, C-ration cans, some helmets and other equipment lay scattered everywhere. The word that came to me was "waste." They had taken the hill. They owned the day. We'd be the small guerilla unit, peering hungrily from the jungle. We would cling to their belt buckle, flow in when they'd left, make do, utilize.

"Take it easy," Jonathan, the Singaporean director, said to me.

"Right. And the American extras are OK?" I asked Bình, the Vietnamese director, for the tenth time. We'd had several problems with the pick-up crew of Europeans we'd used before to play American GIs.

"No problem, I told you. I arranged for them from the university. They're all one group of students."

"Any black guys?"

He hesitated. "There, the bus is pulling up. You can see for yourself."

I walked over, my feet squelching through the mud. It was raining softly but steadily. Bình and Jon picked up helmet liners and clapped them on their heads. The script and costume women were wearing floppy green NVA jungle hats and had draped themselves in plastic bags; they looked layered and awkward as armadillos. Our sneakers or shoes were being encased in gobs of red mud that made you feel you were walking on a planet with twice the normal gravity of Earth: more than the uniforms and dripping metal weapons, it sucked me back to the war.

The extras were climbing off the bus, smiling, blinking. They were the right age, haircuts were good, but they were all white. Damn it,

Bình, I thought. They stood in the mud, joking with each other. I couldn't understand a word they were saying.

"Good morning," I said, to a tall blond boy. He looked at me blankly. Another, shorter, but with a square, all-American face—even, handsome features, very blue eyes—grinned sardonically at me.

"Good morning, Vietnam!" he called to me, in an accent I couldn't place.

"Where are you guys from?"

"We guys!" He seemed delighted with the phrase. "We guys are from Russia. The former Soviet Union," he coaxed, seeing my face. "Your enemies. 'The little commie bastards.'" He laughed, called out something to the others, who laughed also.

I stared at them. Oh shit, Bình. Russians.

We herded them into the small stone hut. The women had carefully kept the same fatigues the European extras had used, and I watched a large Russian put on a shirt with a faded black eagle, globe and anchor on its breast pocket. Where did they manufacture jungle utilities? Some mill town in Massachusetts or Ohio or Tennessee, now gone to dot com businesses or economic depression? When we'd first arrived at Okinawa, we'd been given green dye for our white underwear, and when we went South—which is what we called going to the war, the same term I'd heard the NVA vets use—we wore those and the regular Marine Corps utilities for a month or so, until the lightweight tropical utilities with the big pockets were issued. Utilities, as in utilized. After a time we got rid of the underwear, and wore only the baggy shirts and trousers, wore them for weeks on end, and they absorbed the fluids of the body, the cells of the skin. Until they became a baggy second skin for some kid, maybe from one of the mill towns that had made them and him. Stripped off when he'd been rotated or medevacked or killed. Kicked and spit on and ripped by an ARVN major, enraged at being abandoned. Found crumpled in a warehouse after the NVA took Danang, and two troopers from the village down the hill here had entered the cool, tin-roofed cavernous space warily, AK's at the ready, and screamed in fright when they saw the legged and armed green shapes, like the ghosts of the old enemy. Pulled on now by kids from Moscow and St. Petersburg, helped by the daughters of men who had once shot at the people wearing them. The long, strange trip itself. I may have said it aloud. The kid I'd taken for the all-American boy—he was completely dressed already, helmet, flak jacket—raised his eyebrows and grinned at me sardonically. "'Is that you, John Wayne?'" he asked, "'Is this me?'"

Full Metal Jacket. 1987. Stanley Kubrick.

"Ex-scuse me sir," a boy called to me. "Must we this?" He hefted a flak jacket at me.

"You bet." I went over and tapped another Russian, who had put on the flak jacket, but had put his web suspenders over it. "No," I said. "Nyet. Listen, Kubrick," I pointed at the all-American Russian, "How 'bout you interpret for me? Tell Ivan here these have to go inside."

"No sweat, GI." He saluted me, snapped his heels together, his eyes glinting.

One of the other Russians was talking nonstop to the others, as if giving them instructions. He was big and had a broad, brutal face, accentuated by a crew cut. When he laughed, there was an edge of cruelty in it. He'd be Big Ivan, the steelworker from Pennsylvania. Who dies, I decided.

I got them outside, lined up in the rain. They looked at each other, laughing. The Vietnamese nearby stopped and stared, as they always did when they saw a squad of American soldiers suddenly standing on that soil.

Jonathan had finished positioning the cameras and came over to inspect the extras. "They look mean," he said.

"They look like Russians. Or the fucking Serb army."

He grinned. "We'll get them muddier. All you white guys look alike-la. Look, first shoot, I want them lying in the ditch," he pointed to the sand-bagged position, "facing that way, towards the hills. Get three or four of them to start there, run across there—by the bamboo fence; we're going to set off some explosions as they go by. They're shooting back towards the mountain as they run, but heading for the ditch, falling back. Everybody shooting like hell."

"Where are the NVA?"

"We got a special border police unit to do it. They're on their way."

"I'll muddy 'em up. The M-16's?"

"On the way-la." He turned. "Sammy! The M-16's."

I herded them over to the sandbag-rimmed depression. An M-2 .50 caliber Browning machine gun was sitting on its tripod at one corner, completely exposed. I called over one of the prop men, and gestured towards a pile of sandbags, pantomimed building a position around the gun. He nodded. When I looked back at the Russians, they were passing a bottle filled with transparent liquid around, drinking deeply, smacking their lips in a way you didn't do with water. I sighed again. Everybody had to live up to his or her own stereotypes.

"Listen, Kubrick," I said. "Tell them to put the vodka away and jump into that water." The center of the red-mud depression was sunken and had filled with rainwater. "Tell them to wallow. You understand wallow?" I mimed rubbing my face and chest with mud.

He snapped me another salute.

"You better salute, you commie bastard," I said, grinning at him.

"Are they going to let us win this time, colonel?" he asked.

Rambo: First Blood Part II, 1985.

"You bet."

One of the Russians whooped and let himself fall backwards into the water. "Him," Jonathan said, coming back over. "That one—let's get him to fall like that during the attack." The other boys were laughing, jumping into the mud, throwing it at each other, smearing it on their faces and clothes. Passing the vodka. A dark-haired boy with glasses, now opaque with mud, had taken one bottle and was pouring it into his canteen.

"Jesus-la," Jonathan said.

"Kubrick!" I called. "Let's get them lined up over here, get their weapons."

"'This is my rifle, this is my gun!'" Kubrick clutched his groin.

"That one speaks English?" said Jonathan.

"In a way. He speaks war movie."

"How's that?"

"He seems to know lines from every Vietnam movie ever made."

Jonathan laughed. "Don't you love this, Wayne-oi? Is there anything better than this?"

We lined them up, facing out towards the northern slopes of the mountain, and Long, the quiet, ex-NVA sapper in charge of ord-nance and special effects—that is, blowing up things—handed each an M-16. I showed them how to keep their elbows up, not down into their waists, the way most people who'd never been trained to shoot tended to hold rifles when they were pretending to shoot. Long had loaded the weapons already. The tall blond boy pointed his barrel at me to ask a question, and Jon and I yelled at him at the same time, to keep it pointing in the same direction. We showed them how to cock the rifles, use the safeties. They shot off a ragged volley of blanks at the mountain. The smell of cordite drifted to me. One rifle had misfired, and Jon was showing the boy how to clear it. He had been, he'd told me, in the Singapore army. Every male in Singapore had to do two years of service, at eighteen, though Jon had been deferred until he was 21, because he'd been at university in the states. After active duty, people had to go to yearly reserve duty, until their fifties—the army, if mobilized, was made up of mixed reserve and regular units. It's like Israel, I'd said to him. Exactly like Israel, he'd grinned. It's mod-eled on their system; we have Israeli military advisors, buy weapons from them. It wasn't surprising, he said—Singapore is a small state surrounded by big, unstable, fanatical Muslim states. Right, Jeffery? Jeffrey Yusuf, the Malaysian DOP, had just smiled at him, pointed his finger like a gun, jerked it back.

"Kubrick," I called. "Tell them to pull back the bolts twice, like this, then pull the trigger, make sure the rifles are clear." I showed him with my hands.

Big Ivan slammed the butt of his rifle against the ground, the shock cocking the weapon, an old trick. He caught me looking at him and grinned, then patted his chest. "Militar Russiya," he said, looking at me disdainfully.

"Animal Mother," Kubrick whispered to me, nodding at him. "He talks the talk, but does he walk the walk?"

Full Metal Jacket again. I finally realized just what he reminded me of. "I think he was in the 25th Platoon," I said. "Just like you."

He looked at me blankly. It was a term he hadn't heard in any movie.

The last time I'd run into the 25th Platoon was in what I'll call the Florida Bar, though it is located in a large Northeastern rust-belt city. I'd gone with two poets, Bill Ehrhart and Dave Connolly, ex-Marine and Army. We'd been invited by a local poet and English professor who was doing Vietnam veterans and Country Joe MacDonald, who was making up for *Fixin' to Die Rag*. The bar was on the edge of the worst part of the city. It had a fenced, grassy 1/4 acre lot behind it, with a little pond and a shrine to the dead, over a miniature Japanese-type bridge. The shrine was the three figures of the Hart statue at the Wall: black, white, and Hispanic GI.

Inside, the smoke was thick as gauze. The walls were crusted with Vietnam War memorabilia: unit patches: 101st Airborne, 173rd Airborne, 1st Infantry, 25th Infantry, 193rd Infantry, 1st Cavalry and more, mostly Army. There were helmets with green side out camouflage covers, flight helmets, baseball caps, and utility covers hanging in racks over the bar, and fastened around it were gold and silver flight crew wings, Combat Infantry Badges, airborne wings. There were 105 mm brass artillery shell casings, M-16's, Ka-bar knives, a collection of P38 ration can openers on key chains, photos of young men in baggy fatigues, holding weapons, a painting of a man in a suit touching his finger to the Vietnam memorial wall which contained a grunt ghost touching him back. I think there were sandbags, though my memories of the evening are thick with gauze also. What else? The artifacts of a museum to perverse nostalgia. A shelf of Zippo lighters, one each, inscribed. *This Marine is Going to Heaven/He Served His Time in Hell. No Mission Too Difficult/No Sacrifice Too Big.* A naked woman bathing in a champagne glass: *When You Can't Be With the One You Love/Kill the One You're With.* One that got to me: *Too Young to Vote/But Not to Die/Too Young to Love/But Too Old to Cry.* T-shirts for sale, mostly POW-MIA: *You're Not Forgotten, They Still Wait,* and *Been There/ Done That.* Above the door, large poster-photos of Westmoreland and Abrams, in tribute, and an equally large photo of Jane Fonda behind an antiaircraft gun in Hanoi, not in tribute. I could say: it was that kind of place, but I'd never seen a place like it, except for a chain of theme restaurants built around the motif of a World War Two bomber squadron O-club. The Idea of the thing: the Vietnam E-club Disney ride, only the animatronic figures might hurt you if you didn't take them seriously.

Some of the clientele were students from the poet's class. Most of the rest had dressed to fit into the décor and reinforce the myth they'd decided to build their identities around, all other options being less interesting. Ponytails, mustaches, black sleeveless leather vests, baseball caps with unit or Veterans' organization patches. *Vietnam Vet and Proud of It. Vietnam: If You Weren't There, Shut Up.* The experience had been anointed by the culture now. But I remembered when many vets would respond to the question of whether they had served in Vietnam by shaking their heads violently, as if to dislodge a word they felt imprinted in red on their foreheads.

"Oh Jesus," Bill said.

"Amen, my brother," said Dave.

Yes, I thought. But wondered if we were any different: three writers still living inside the war.

On the right side of the room were several overstuffed armchairs and sofas, the armrests black with grease stains, yellowish cotton erupting from tears in the upholstery. We got beers and struggled over, sat on one, the cushions sagging under us. Waves of noise from the small stage at the back of the bar blasted my ears, the music intertwining with snatches of war stories. You remember that seven-toed dink in Quảng Bình? Swing with the Wing. What do they know, even the women and kids, booby-trapped, broken glass up the wazoo, right after all, lookit the boat people, we ran that orphanage, least we could do, heh-heh. Two tall lean men, both with black Bruce Springsteen goatees and baseball caps, were sitting across from us. Connolly asked them what outfit they'd been in, found out it was his brigade. They began throwing names and places at each other. One rolled a doobie, lit it, inhaled deeply, offered it around. Hey man, be cool, his friend said. I fought for my country and I can smoke dope any fucking place I want, the first said. Bill seemed paralyzed, staring into the space directly in front of his eyes, as if he'd convinced himself he was invisible. The only way to deal with this, I understood, was to be as drunk as possible as soon as possible. I began ordering boilermakers. The faces around me grew red-lit, saturnine, their edges trailing into smoke. There was a certain amount of border blending. Country Joe got up, and began the chant and the anthem. He asked everyone to give him an F, and they obliged, gave him the U, the C, the K, anything he wanted. Who were these people, the Woodstock generation or the boys from Mỹ Lai? Maybe that was the secret, no difference, we are all one.

And it's one, two, three
What are we fighting for
Don't ask me, 'cause I don't give a damn
Next stop is Vietnam

The mouths in the faces were all opening, lips forming the words. The grunts reflected in the black Vietnam memorial, touching their brothers' hands on the outside, suddenly came through the wall, filed onto the lawn, into the bar, filthy, smelly, web gear dangling, weapons at the ready, stopped, looked around in anguish, and screamed, *We really can never go back to the World.* I suddenly understood what had happened, where I was. The plane had gone down on the way here. This was my afterlife. I was stuck forever in the Florida Bar. For my sins.

Ain't no time to ask us why
Whoopee! We're all gonna die.

A tall fat white man in a black sateen jacket with a Military Police badge on it was lecturing Ehrhart. "No, man, Westmoreland is so underrated." A tall thin black man was standing in front of Connolly, swaying slightly, glaring down at him. His eyes were wrong. He put his hand in his pocket. I gripped my beer bottle. I saw Ehrhart do the same.

"You weren't there at all, you google-eyed freak, were you?" the black man said to Connolly. "You never killed no little gook babies."

Connolly, it's true, looks, at some angles, like Mr. Peepers. It's deceptive. He's South Boston Irish and very tough, and he had been there enough to literally have his guts shot out. Blown off a half-track by an NVA RPG, as he lay on the ground, watching his intestines spill out into the dirt, he'd seen an NVA with an AK47 pop out of a spider hole inside the perimeter, between Connolly and the rest of his squad, their backs to him, and Connolly unable to move, unable to shoot, hardly able to scream, had to watch as the NVA killed all his friends. In the anti-war movement, he'd been known also for his fearlessness and the fierceness of his opposition to the war—he came from a family of IRA supporters and descendants, as well as from a family that was working class and conscious of it in a way that probably doesn't exist anywhere else in America anymore as it does in Boston. At some point during the war, he became convinced that the working class was being slaughtered for interests not its own, and that, going through the villages, he felt like a British Black and Tan.

He wasn't, I wanted to tell the black vet, someone to fuck with. The man was glaring down at him. "You left me in the zone, you Jody motherfucker," he said. "Lying there and the chopper came in, and you took all the ofays and left the brothers behind. Left me bleeding. No Viet Cong ever called me nigger."

He pulled his hand out of his pocket. He had a razor blade in it. Bill and I started to rise, our hands clutching the beer bottles. The vet with the doobie took his arm, put the joint in his mouth. "Hey, bro', he ain't who you think he is. Come on down. Welcome home, man."

The man looked around wildly. "Saigon, shit, I'm still in Saigon," he muttered.

Ehrhart jerked his head around to look at him, a light shining in his eyes. "What outfit were you in?" he asked. The man looked at him disdainfully.

"The 25th Platoon, you honky motherfucker," he said proudly. The three of us looked at each other. No one would name an outfit he'd served with that way. At the least it would be company, battalion, regiment, division. Or squadron, group, wing. He walked off. A minute later, he was confronting someone else, across the bar, the razor in his hands.

"How did you know?" Connolly asked Bill.

"Shit, every word he said was from some movie or other."

"If you weren't there," the ponytailed vet with the joint in his mouth said sadly, "shut the fuck up."

• • •

We ran the Russians all morning: dry runs, where they would just pretend to fire, and then live-fire takes. The second scene would involve six extras crouching in the sandbag-rimmed crater; we'd use four M-16s on full automatic and the machine gun firing out at invisible NVA. To simulate mortar rounds coming in, Mr. Long, our ex NVA sapper, had buried TNT charges packed in canvas bags—they were literally satchel charges without the shrapnel, a few yards out. I explained where everyone would go to Kubrick, asked him if he understood. He nodded.

"All I ask of any man is he get his ass out in the grass with the rest of us," he said.

"Rambo?"

He looked offended. *"Hamburger Hill."*

A small olive-green truck pulled up next to the stone hut where we'd dressed the boys. The back gate popped down, and Vietnamese in green pith helmets and fatigues began jumping down, two, then four, six, ten—and it was suddenly clowns in the circus, an impossible number piling from the tiny car, and it seemed they would never stop, they would keep coming, overrun us; one horde to each truck, I'd finally cracked the secret of the Hồ Chí Minh Trail. Twelve, fourteen, twenty. Jonathan was laughing, shaking his head. "How the hell did they pack them in like that?" When they were out, and lined up, I saw they were the right age—late teens and early twenties, though they looked younger. As was right. But the green pith helmets were clean, and their fatigues looked too new, pressed, bright. "No, don't worry," Bình said to me. "They're police, how do you say, for the border. We have old uniforms and sandals for them." He waved at the two women who were descending on the boys.

After they were dressed and armed, the Russians came over, and the two groups switched weapons—AK47's for M-16's—and posed with each other. Looking at them, I felt nothing. It would have been more resonant, I thought, if the Western extras were American kids—descendants of the combatants meeting to commemorate their fathers' war, instead of to kill each other. As it were it looked like a ragtag group of Balkan guerillas from one faction or another, strangely reinforced by volunteers from the old North Vietnamese Army.

Afterwards, one of the Vietnamese kids, perhaps inspired by the clothing, began practicing a low crawl, through some concertina wire. I watched. It was the crawl of song and legend, though a real sapper would have come through the wire naked and greased and hung with bandoleers packed with plastique. But the kid knew what he was doing, had clearly been trained. Each move was deliberate, a series of short jerks, elbow, elbow, knee, knee, that flowed together, and he moved over the ground as silently and smoothly as conscious water.

I brought Big Ivan and five others over to the pit and got them set up.

"OK, on 'action' you're shooting over there—the NVA are coming right at you. Come on, translate, Kubrick! After a moment, you'll hear the director yell fire! Don't hesitate, put your faces down. Later, we'll film you going over backwards. You got it? Kubrick, tell Ivan there if he keeps sucking that bottle, he's out."

Ivan shot me a murderous look.

"Pay attention," I said. "You keep your head up, you may lose it."

I positioned them on the inside of the sandbags, their feet in the mud puddle behind them.

"Smoke," Bình yelled, and Hung, our smoke machine, lit the tar mixture he'd put into a basket on the end of a twelve-foot pole, and ran back and forth in front of the perimeter, sweeping the basket. Bình yelled something, and Hung ran over to camera A, let the smoke billow in front of the lens.

"OK," Jon yelled. "Roll A, roll B! Action!"

They began shooting fiercely, the echoes rolling off the hills. I saw one of the M-16's wasn't firing. The tall blond who'd asked me about the flak jacket—raised the weapon and looked questioningly at the camera.

"Cut!" Jon yelled. "Tell him just to pretend shoot-la. No matter."

On the next take, the boy pointed his rifle at the hill and pretended to squeeze the trigger, and made shooting noises with his mouth. You couldn't hear, but understood clearly, from the way his lips moved, that he was saying "ka-chew, ka-chew."

"Cut!" Jon yelled. "Tell him to stop that." I nodded to Kubrick. When the firing had begun, he had seemed to freeze. He was looking off into the hills now, seeing who knew which war movie. "Kubrick," I said again, and he nodded and yelled something to the boy. The other Russians snickered. "Ka-chew, ka-chew," they chorused. Big Ivan looked disgusted. "OK, one more time," Jon yelled. "Roll A, roll B. Action! . . . no, cut, cut!"

"Kubrick," I said. "He's still doing it. Tell him not to."

Kubrick went over to the boy, put his hand on his shoulder, looked him in the eye.

"Yuri," he said gently, and then a stream of Russian, of which I understood, "Nyet," and "ka-chew." Yuri nodded.

They're children, I thought, and it wasn't the thought or what it evoked so much as the words themselves that seemed to freeze in my chest. The explosion caught me unaware: I hadn't even heard Jon's shout. The shock slapped at me, and a few clods of dirt pelted my face and shoulders. When I turned around, Mr. Long was grinning at me.

"Missed again, you fuck," I told him. I pointed my finger in his direction. "Ka-chew, ka-chew."

"Ka-chew, ka-chew," the Russians echoed behind me.

When I looked over for Kubrick, I saw him squatting behind the umbrella set up over camera A. His hands were trembling slightly and he was very pale. "You OK? Kubrick?"

"Never get off the fucking boat," he said.

It rained off and on all day, only letting up into a trailing mist that filmed dramatically, but chilled to the bone. The Russians had poured the vodka into their canteens, and would take long, gulping drinks whenever there was a lull in the shooting. It seemed to make them happier, with the exception of Big Ivan, who became more and more surly. After Sammy's explosions, he and the others were to lie in the mud puddle, dead. As Sương, one of the wardrobe women, bent over Ivan, painting on blood, he clutched her ankle, and began groping up her leg. She smiled and shook her head, as if to say, what can you expect from GIs?

"Cut it out, Big Ivan," I yelled to him.

He sat up and glared at me. "Nyet 'Big Ivan.' Fyodor. You say— Fyodor." He thumped his chest again. "Militar Russiya. Good. Militar Americansky, Vietnam. Shit. *Scheiss*. You understand?"

"Afghanistan," I said to him. "Now lie down and be dead."

Kubrick said something to him sharply, and he lay down. He seemed to obey Kubrick; they all did.

We shot three more firefight segments, using both the "Americans" and the Vietnamese. For the last scene, everyone would be dead; it would be a first for Vietnamese cinema, Bình told me. In the past, they had never been permitted to show the dead from their side. We arranged them in the mud, smoke rising in columns from burning tires all around them: a GI body here, a Vietnamese body there; sometimes only one, sometimes in clusters, sometimes entwined with each other. The reality would have been more like hamburger, but the smoke and mist and mud and fires; the uniforms and equipment and faces and where we were made it real enough, or at least representative enough, and for a second I had to turn away. They were children.

Big Ivan suddenly rose from the dead. He was shaking his head. "Nyet, nyet," he said, and shot a stream of Russian at Kubrick. I looked at him.

"He says it only looks like a movie. He says he was in the Russian army, he can tell you how to do it. He's drunk."

It was the first time Kubrick had replied to me in straight language. His voice was strained with a disproportionate anger. I started to say something, but before I could, Kubrick began shouting. His face was pale in the mist, and I saw his hands were trembling, as they had been after the explosions. The big Russian put his head down, hangdog, like a scolded child, his size making it somehow more pathetic. He lay back down again.

"What did you say to him?" I asked Kubrick. He was still angry, very pale, his small, thin body trembling, and I thought I saw his eyes glistening. As I watched he came back to himself, shook his head. "His ass," he said, "was never in the grass."

I looked away for a second, at the field of the dead, Kubrick looking with me, still trembling slightly. Something occurred to me. "Chechnya?" I asked him. For a second, I thought I saw him flinch. Then he grinned at me, his eyes bright, his face suddenly skullish in the gray light, and shook his head vehemently.

NESTING

"MY HEBREW NAME IS YOSSI ALSO," BRIAN SCHULMAN explained to his son.

"Yossi and Yossi. Boy that's dumb," Tim said.

The echo of the names caught in Brian's mind. When he'd first come back from Vietnam, he'd gone to live for a time in Israel; while he was there he had gradually come to think of himself by his Hebrew name. Now, some twenty years later, his Israeli cousin, just out of the army, had shown up large as life at his Maryland door and introduced himself by the same name: his own younger self dropping in for a visit. Brian, an archaeologist, found he distrusted the symmetry of the occasion; he'd never liked the kind of theoretical work that slid the patterns of the present over the past like a transparency.

"What kind of name is 'Teem'?" his cousin asked, drawing out the word. "Like a football team?" He watched Yossi reach over and rough Tim's hair. Tim grinned. Brian felt a little relieved. The boy, eight years old, usually adopted a teasing, sarcastic manner toward relatives who would overly praise his cuteness or smartness, exaggerate their pleasure at being in his presence. His attitude sometimes pleased Brian, as if his son was an imp—a secret name—he could free from his heart to say the things he no longer dared or could afford to say. Sometimes. But now he was afraid Yossi would just see a spoiled American brat.

"It's Tim. T-I-M. And why's Dad need an Israeli name anyway?"

Yossi shrugged.

Tim peered at him doubtfully. "Do you know how to play Metroid?"

"Sure."

"You know how?"

"Yes, of course."

"Tim, Yossi just got here," Brian said. "We've hardly had a chance to talk."

"You mean Yossi wants to talk to Yossi," Tim teased.

"I don't mind," Yossi said, something in his voice reminding Brian of the relief it had been to play with the kids when he'd come to stay with Yossi's parents, a break from their kind but relentless interrogation about his parents, his service in the American military.

"Go ahead," he said. "But just for a few minutes, Tim."

Tim led Yossi to his room. In a minute, Brian heard the electronic bleeping of the game. In the paper a few days before, he'd read about an American immigrant to Israel who'd introduced a video game based on the intifada: you blipped little running Palestinians. He put up some coffee and sat down on the couch, listening to Tim's excited voice. What's your name, cousin? Yossi's father Danny had asked him, when he'd arrived at his cousin's house on the moshav.

Brian.

No, *b'ivrit*, in Hebrew. Not your American name. Your Jewish name.

Yosef. After my grandfather, Brian had said. Yosef was the root from which his paternal family, in America and Israel, branched—his parents had been immigrants, fleeing the pogroms in Poland years before the Holocaust had wiped out any relatives that remained: Brian, his American name, he suspected, had been given both as a hope and as camouflage.

Twenty years ago, Danny had grinned and kissed his son's stomach. Like this one, he'd said. Yossi and Yossi. Then he winked, encompassing Brian into a mutual history. The Yosef both Yossi and he were named after was a pious Jew who had had to kill a Polish deserter who was threatening his family. Yosef had hit the man with a frozen branch, but the act of violence, according to Brian's mother, was so abhorrent to his nature that his own body punished him shortly afterwards with a stroke, the arm he had used to wield the branch going dead, frozen. When, in the war, Brian heard men speak of the Vietnamese as animal-like, dirty, indifferent to death and easy to kill, he'd stood back from them inside his parents', Yosef's, understanding: he couldn't even bring himself to use the word gook. Of course his moral fastidiousness didn't last; it wasn't the kind of war where it could. When he had finally allowed himself to hate as well as kill, he'd felt nothing more than relief, the elation of a Cossack. But still, in Vietnam his Jewishness, Yosef's eyes behind his own, had made him feel an outsider; having been in Vietnam he felt outside the Jews, outside, for that matter, most Americans.

Now Danny's son, Yosef's other namesake, came back into his living room and sat silently on his couch, burly as his father, but his hair black and cropped short, coarser, his eyebrows heavier, eyes lidded and duller, movements slower: he had Danny's strength, but the air of combative, intelligent ambiguity, the slight awkwardness of a saving, sardonic doubt or shame about his own strength, his ability to perform violence with great competence that Danny had held in the tilt of his head and in the twinkle of his eyes, was missing, as if strained at last from this generation.

Sara entered, and Yossi held out his hand awkwardly. Sara shook it and smiled politely and asked about his trip. Brian was suddenly aware of the smell of stale sweat, an acrid foreignness intruding into the small room. He could see a faint twitch of distress, a tightness in Sara's face that he found he resented; Yossi had been on the road, what did she expect?

"Would you like to take a shower before dinner?" she asked.

"That's all right," Yossi said.

They were snagged in a silence. Brian looked at his wife, reading her annoyance at this intrusion, her Lutheran wariness: Yossi, darkly hirsute, thick set, standing in his comfortable, utterly self-possessed Israeli silence, was the child of a choice Brian had almost made.

"You just got out of the army?"

"Yes?" Yossi said, his response a surprised question, an Israeli way that brought Brian back again.

"When I first went to Israel," he said, "I was about your age. Just out of the army, like you, and I wanted to travel, not be tied down. It was just after the war."

"Yes, my father told me."

"You were just a baby. But now you've been a soldier too."

Yossi let another silence gather between them.

"Blech, blech, blech," Tim said, imitating the gutturals of the Hebrew.

"Did you go to Europe?" Brian asked.

Yossi looked questioningly at him, and he realized he'd asked the question in English.

"A little. But I wanted to come here. For Israelis, we like to come to the United States." He waved helplessly. "The movies."

"Has it been like the movies?"

"You know, only this place." Yossi's smile was a surprise; it made his face look animated and intelligent. "Little houses, fields, the river. Like the United States of the movies."

"This area always reminded me of the Jezreel. Or the Bet Shean, near your moshav."

Yossi snorted. "No, I don't think so."

They looked away from each other to the blank television screen, as if seeing what connected them on it, flowing to join under the glass of the set. Yossi got up suddenly, squatted in front of the set and pulled the on switch. The sudden light flickered into a commercial, then the news theme. Brian feared what pictures would appear next, flare out of their minds onto the screen: soldiers with clubs, rock-throwing children; there had been coverage of the Palestinian uprising almost every night this week. He pictured his cousin, the Jewish Cossack finally constructed, his face masked by a plastic visor, his arm swinging in wild arcs against dark, scattering forms.

Yossi reached over and switched off the television, as if he had shared Brian's fear.

"Where were you?" Brian asked. "In the army?"

"Somewhere in Israel." Yossi grinned at his own use of the stock phrase, the smile again emerging like a hidden person under the sheened blankness of the visor.

"And in the territories?" Brian insisted. "The intifada?"

"It's a complicated situation," Yossi said.

Brian snorted. Yossi looked down, a student who had given the wrong answer.

"Maybe not so complicated," Brian said, then felt disgusted with himself at baiting this boy—he hadn't the right, hadn't chosen to live in Israel, be Yossi; he'd become Brian, bunkered in here in the United States of the movies.

"You were in the Israeli army, huh?" Tim said. "Wow, like I'm really impressed."

Brian gave Tim a look. He made a face, his father's own expression exaggerated in miniature. Yossi reached over and rumpled the boy's hair. Brian felt a twinge of panic—Yossi's large, capable hand, a soldier's hand, moving toward the boy—that surprised and shamed him.

Yossi was still looking at the floor. Startled, Brian saw that his Israeli cousin's eyes had brimmed with tears.

Sara trailed her hand down his chest. "There weren't any tears. You just saw yourself, your own compassion."

"Is that what it was?"

"Why is it so important to you that I like him?"

There was a business card on the night table, propped against the base of the lamp. Brian picked it up and looked at it.

"How long will he stay?" Sara asked.

"I'm not sure."

"Why don't you just come out and ask him?"

"Asking him when he's leaving is like asking him to leave."

"My God, Brian."

"The funny thing is, if I were Israeli, I probably wouldn't think twice about asking, being that blunt," he said. "But still, I lived for months with his parents; I was never asked that question." Then he said, to her look: "Oh, I don't mean he'll be here for months."

He turned the card between his fingers. "Did the broker call today?"

"No, not yet. It's part of the whole ceremony. The twisting in the wind. To be sure we're worthy."

He looked at the card. On one side was a list of names. If he had questions, he was to talk to Julie for inquiries about scheduling and costs, Kristen for disbursements, Susan for escrow releases, Tuyết for payments. For what things cost. The Sisters of Our Lady of Equity. Tuyết. The one Vietnamese name, complete with diacritics, stood out, encompassed yet there, in his Maryland bedroom.

"When are we worthy?" he asked.

"You're never sure. That's part of the ceremony too." She took the card from him and looked at the names. "You know what he's saying here? Don't bother me, I have women to handle the shit work. You notice he never talks to me when we're in the office. It's like you're applying for a mortgage yourself."

Lately Brian had been waking up in the middle of the night, worried about getting the mortgage, putting what was around them, the walls of the bunker, into their name. A familiar panic would scramble in his chest and he'd be fully awake, sweating, as if he had heard mortars falling outside, shaking the walls. They were renting the house with an option, but the loan officer had been very cautious—with both their incomes they made enough to qualify, but they owed many debts: he wasn't sure they could make the payments.

"See Tuyết for payments," he said.

Sara moved her hand onto her belly, as if to show what had been paid.

"I'm sorry," he said.

She closed her eyes. "I dreamt it was a girl," she said. "Dreamt I saw her face at our window. Out in the dark."

He knew Sara was speaking about her miscarriage; it had only been a month ago, but for some reason, the word "girl," he supposed, he thought of Amy Hayden, his neighbor Carol Hayden's daughter; she'd been molested by another neighbor, a farmer named Johns who'd befriended the family. Carol, a divorcee, was afraid the man would get away with it because he was from an old county family. Brian felt the same twist of fear and cold rage in his chest now that he'd felt when he'd first heard of Johns's arrest, the reason for it, Johns's closeness to their house: he'd wanted to erase Johns, literally blot him from the same world where Tim lived. He didn't say anything to Sara now. She'd lost the child shortly after the incident with Johns and she hated to talk about the molestations.

"It wasn't a girl," he said. "It wasn't anything yet."

"It was. She was." Sara took his hand, pressed it against her stomach. Against the absence. "She was, she would have been. I know. I carried her. That's where the term comes from."

"Maybe it's because I didn't feel it, her, in me," Brian said. "When you were pregnant with Tim, he was nothing to me. An abstraction. But then an hour after he was born, I knew I'd die for him, die protecting him. I'd certainly kill for him. Yet before he was here, I couldn't imagine feeling like that."

She ran a finger over his cheek, to his lips.

"What a strange way to put it. I don't think of dying for Tim—the opposite. I mean, I would, I'd 'die for him'," she said the phrase as if it were in quotation marks. "But I don't think of it that way."

"Would you kill for him?"

She looked at him oddly. He heard a noise, an alien shuffle, in the hall.

"At least there's someone here for Tim," he said.

"What a funny thing to say, Brian." She turned over on her side, away from him.

He turned off the light. He remembered that another neighbor, Louise Hallam, a counselor at a home for troubled girls, had told him she had a client, a Vietnamese girl; her father was a black GI. The kid had been found living on the street, on drugs, abused; the girl didn't know who she was, Louise had said, though she'd used some sort of counselor terminology, something about a lack of self-image. He didn't think they were called troubled girls anymore either. In the dark now, in his sleepy brain, Louise's Vietnamese girl trembled into Amy Hayden, into *Tuyết*, self-images confused: troubled girls, troubling girls hovering near his windows, peering in, scratching at the glass. Begging for his protection. He flowed out of the house, going through the woods to Johns's house. Over the hills and through the woods. Here I am. He'd probably killed or helped to kill better people in Vietnam. No, not probably. He heard the soft shuffle from the hall again and he coaxed open the front door, pushed against it with his mind, and let Yossi, a silent, helmeted golem, slip out, sent him spinning to Johns. Yossi's face, the twisted malevolent face he pictured under the rim of the helmet was, he realized, a Nazi caricature of a Jew. He lowered the plastic visor so there was no face and only the reflected face of the moon and he saw Tuyết's face, saw it as if it was the face of his own unborn daughter, named and emerging from the green jungle as she caught sight of Yossi and Yossi, silent twins moving toward her through the trees; he saw her face fall into fright, he saw her run.

"Were you and Yossi's father in the war together?"

"A war happened when I was in Israel, but I wasn't in it. Do you know the difference between Israel and Vietnam?"

He saw Tim flinch and he heard the edge in his voice. Tim said, "You won't let me see *Platoon* or rent the game."

"What's that have to do with it?"

"Woody's dad lets him get it."

"Is your name Woody?"

"How long will he stay?" Tim asked.

"Do you like him?"

"He's strong."

"What kind of answer is that?"

Tim shrugged. "He wrestles with me. What are you doing today?"

"I'm going to take him out to the dig. Want to come?"

Brian was drinking coffee and looking out of the window. Sparrows were landing on the lawn, spilling in an arc from the sky. They kept coming, as if they were being poured, scattering over an acre of ground, pecking, feeding. The lawn had been mown short. Yossi, he realized, must have done it yesterday; he had quietly taken over the yard work. The morning air, coming in through the kitchen window, had a rich cut-grass smell. Brian saw a rabbit dart across the lawn and into the tangled jungle of ivy and wild roses that grew between the screen of locust trees along the road. Their leaves moved in a breeze that came in a second to his skin, the land that would go in his name spreading flat and to the trees, an empty, close-cut space on which he could easily spot movement, the flicker of a rabbit, the approach of an enemy.

"Nope," Tim said.

"Why not?"

Tim shrugged again. "Are you going to get me a tape today?"

"You have to do more this weekend than watch tapes and play Nintendo. Are you reading anything?"

"*The Lion, the Witch and the Wardrobe*."

"Again?"

"I like it."

Tim looked at Brian. "Pick me up, Dad."

"You're too big."

"Pick me up."

He took his son under the armpits and held him up, Tim's arms going around his neck, legs wrapping around his waist, the warm weight of him. He wondered how long he'd have this. When Sara would be on night duty at the hospital and they were alone in the house, Tim would crawl into bed and snuggle into Brian's back and he'd read to him from the Chronicles of Narnia about how human children, the sons of Adam and the daughters of Eve, went through the darkness in the back of the closet into a bright kingdom where they battled evil, a place where evil and time and death could be defeated. He pressed Tim to him and kissed the top of his head.

"Mushers," Tim said.

"Go get Yossi up."

"I thought you were Yossi."

"So go tell Yossi that Yossi wants him."

"You're weird, Dad."

"So do you want to go to the dig with us?"

"No."

"Why not?"

"It's boring."

The dig didn't move Yossi either. The sites Brian had worked on in Israel when he'd first become interested in archaeology were more ancient and he supposed, to the layman, more dramatic. The dig here was at the site of a Civil War POW camp; they were sinking trenches into the hospital and graveyard areas. Old fraggings. Thousands of Confederate prisoners had died of starvation or abuse or plain murder, their bodies dumped everywhere, their bones laced under the earth. There had been a regiment of black guards at Point Lookout, an element of payback that had initially hooked Brian's interest: victims creating victims, people who had had terrible things done to them feeling licensed to do terrible things to others, the whole cycle in microcosm.

Watching the other volunteers dig, seeing what emerged from the solid earth under their feet, his cousin Yossi remained silent, almost militantly noncommittal, as if to say this was not his ground, not his crime.

Brian showed Yossi the boat he was trying to get into shape, a fourteen-foot oak and cedar Old Town, trimmed with Philippine mahogany. He'd spotted it rotting outside a barn in Chopticon and paid the farmer who owned it fifty dollars. He had it up on a trailer next to his shed now. The two of them were standing looking at it when Alex Hallam, the county sheriff, pulled up.

"You going to get yourself out on the water, Brian?"

"Part of my assimilation campaign; Jordy Hewitt"—Brian named a waterman who lived nearby—"calls me 'that digging and drawing and writing fella.' He grins and shakes his head when he says it, as if he can't figure how I get by like that, without doing any real work."

Alex nodded at Yossi. Brian introduced him.

"Where you from, Hossi," Alex said, shaking his hand.

"Israel."

"Yossi just got out of the army. He's a farmer," Brian felt compelled to tell Alex, as if to say we're not all drawing and writing and accounting and lawyering fellas.

Alex grunted, as if withholding judgment.

Brian patted the boat. "I want to sand the bottom, caulk it, paint it. But first we need to get it off the trailer and upside down."

Yossi went into the shed. In a minute he came out, carrying two small sawhorses, then two more. He went back in and came out with several two-by-fours, Brian's tool set. Brian watched Alex watching Yossi. His cousin quickly and efficiently lined up and nailed a board between two sawhorses. Brian fixed up the other set and they put them next to the boat, while Alex rummaged around, came out with the varnish, caulk and anti-fouling paint.

"Heavy boat," he said to Yossi.

Yossi did his shrug. He fingered the metal rope loop at the bow, walked to the stem, and touched the loops there.

"Do you have two long *ahmodim* . . . how do you say, sticks?"

"There's some old poles behind the shed."

Yossi got them, then tapped the loops. He pantomimed levering the boat over.

They slid the poles through. Brian got ready to turn the boat, but he saw Alex looking oddly at Yossi. Yossi stared thoughtfully at the boat.

Brian wondered what both of them saw—he felt outside of whatever was passing between them. Yossi walked over to the hinged, glassless windshield and pulled it out. He swung it back and forth in its arc. A slight grin fluttered on Alex's lips. Yossi took the coil of rubberized clothesline Brian had in the toolbox and lashed the windshield to its frame. When they turned the boat over, Brian saw now, the windshield would have swung out and hit the ground. It was the kind of detail he wouldn't have thought of anymore; except for digging into the past his hands no longer worked with the solid objects of the world, knew what they could cost. He saw Alex catch Yossi's eye and nod at him as if he'd passed a test Brian hadn't even known was going on.

"What's up?" Brian asked. He was used to Alex dropping over; they were neighbors. When they'd first met, Alex, in a friendly, howdy-neighbor conversation, had put Brian through a subtly efficient interrogation about his background, finding out, among other things, that they'd both been in the war the same year, though Alex in the Marines, Brian in the Army. They'd been friends, or at least friendly, since. But Alex was in uniform today and, Brian presumed, on duty.

"I need to ask you again—did Tim have any contact with Johns?"

"I'd have told you if he did, Alex."

"Have you noticed anybody you don't know in the area, intruders, anyone unusual?"

Brian laughed. "No. At least not any more unusual than usual. What's going on?"

"Johns has disappeared. His barn's been burned down."

"Maybe he did it himself. Ran away."

"We've had that thought. I hope it's true."

Brian felt a stab of anger at Alex's protectiveness. Johns was from an old county family like Alex's, his behavior had probably been overlooked for years, a *droit du seigneur* long practiced until an outsider complained. "Or maybe someone fragged him," he said. "I hope so."

"Maybe," Alex said. "But you don't want to be saying things like that."

"Not to the county sheriff?"

"Not to anyone. I know who you are, Brian. I'm not Jordy Hewitt—you don't need to impress me."

Later, thinking of Alex Hallam's visit, looking at Yossi working in the garden, an idea formed in Brian's mind: a thought sliding by that at first he didn't want to stop and hold. What if Yossi had done it, killed Johns? It was a mind game, Brian understood that, but it seized him strongly. He remembered his fantasy the night he'd talked about Johns with Sara. Yossi stood hunched over the Rototiller now, hulking and silent and blank, a part of Brian come back, a golem he might have set loose with the force of his hate for Johns; Yossi's hands still competent and at ease with the arcs of violence in the world. Yet, he told himself uneasily, surprised at himself for starting to look at ways this fantasy would, could actually be possible, for needing to reassure himself, yet Yossi was changing, becoming more animated, smiling more frequently, acting out for Brian the same healing metamorphosis he had thought to enact when he'd stayed with Yossi's parents.

For the most part, his cousin stayed around the house, playing with Tim, working in the garden the way Brian had worked his father's land twenty years before. He brought the Rototiller Brian had given up on back to life and churned the soil in the thirty-by-fifty plot, furrowing vertically and then horizontally and then diagonally, crossing and crisscrossing until the soil threatened to become fine as sand and Brian had to call him in and say *maspeek*, Yossi, enough, rest. Brian had even started to rely on him to be with Tim. The boy was eight, an age when he saw his neighbors' kids walk or bike over on their own to each other's houses; he'd considered it a safe area before Johns's arrest; that was one reason they lived there, and even now he knew Tim still had to learn to be independent. But he was worried whenever Tim went out on his own and now if he or Sara were at work, at least he knew that

Yossi would be with Tim, playing video games, wrestling. Although he understood Sara's objection—it was like having two kids in the house. What if he'd somehow communicated his fear of Tim being in this area where Johns was to Yossi? Might that not be a reason, a motive? Stop it, he told himself. Seeing Tim's lit-up face, hearing his shrieks of delight as Yossi tossed him, swung him upside down, Sara, Brian felt, was warming to his cousin. Yet what if her apprehension were right, some mother's instinct telling her something was off here.

Mad vet flips out. Stop it.

On Tuesday evening, when she was at work, Brian fixed hot dogs and beans and they sat in front of the television, watching cartoons. "It's a boys' night," he explained to Tim, who was delighted at the idea. Brian cleared the dishes from the folding tables. When he returned from the kitchen, he saw that Yossi's face had changed, gone to the set dullness of those first days; his cousin sat slumped on the couch, his hands dangling between his knees. On the screen were the images they had tried to banish from the house: the hate-twisted faces of rock-throwing children, soldiers charging with arcing, falling clubs that they wielded like heavy branches, their arms strained finally of Grandpa Yosef's weakness. Brian looked away, inadvertently catching Yossi's eye as he did, and their gazes slid past each other, Yossi looking away from Yossi.

His cousin wiped his face. Tim looked at him, then got up and turned off the television. He went over to Yossi.

"Look strong."

Yossi grinned blankly. "What?"

"Look strong. You know." Tim snapped into a muscleman pose. "Make a muscle."

Yossi made a muscle, a grin twisting his face, lighting it oddly. Tim's finger shot toward his armpit, tickling. Yossi grabbed the boy and swung him up over his head, the swishing arc of the motion slicing at Brian's heart, Tim's skull brushing sickeningly close to the ceiling. Yossi swung the boy upside down, Tim's face close, too close to the floor and now Brian's Israeli cousin, laughing, grabbed his son and swung him up to his shoulder and over and down, thudding him onto the rug, Yossi's face suffused with light, and Brian was on his feet suddenly, grabbing the bunched power of his cousin's arm, the massive, sweated muscle twitching under his palm, and he yelled, "Cut it out, Yossi, enough."

The animation drained from Yossi's face, leaving a dull passive mask with wounded eyes. He shambled from the room.

Tim stared after him, his eyes filming. "Sometimes you're such a dork, Dad," he said.

The next day, Brian brewed coffee and read the paper in the quiet of the morning. Yossi was up; he could hear the noises he made in his room. When he came out, Brian smiled at him and Yossi smiled back weakly, but his eyes still fled and when Brian asked him if he wanted coffee, he shook his head. A moment later the sound of a motor broke the morning. When Brian looked out of the window he saw Yossi behind the tiller, moving back and forth, trapped in the square of the garden patch.

The dock Brian used was on the eastern side of the ten-acre meadow bordering the rear of their lot: the meadow ended in a wooded slope that went down to the creek, an estuary off the Potomac. The land was once part of a tobacco farm bought by the same developer who was selling the Schulmans the house; when more families moved in they would have sharing rights on the dock, but meanwhile the meadow and the dock were Brian's and that day Yossi and Tim and he walked through the Johnson grass and Queen Anne's lace and late-blooming flowers to the water. Tim walked between them, holding their hands, and they lifted him so his feet flew above the meadow. "Higher, Yossi and Yossi," he shouted. When they brought him down, walking between them fast, Yossi stuck his leg out in front of Tim so that the boy sprawled, laughing. "Daddy, he's torturing me, he's an Israeli torturer," Tim yelled, bounding up, and Brian tripped him also.

"Yossi and Yossi," Tim said from the ground, "suck." Brian looked at Yossi and they both grinned.

"Where'd you pick up that language, champ?"

"What language?"

Yossi grabbed Tim under his arms, Brian took his legs, Yossi and Yossi holding the boy. They swung him back and forth, threatening to send him flying into the sea of wildflowers, as Tim shrieked with delight.

It was past the legal season, but the unusually warm weather had kept crabs in the creek. At the dock, Tim showed Yossi how to chicken-neck. He made him pull in the trot lines as he stood poised at the edge with a dip net. "No, Yossi, slower. Don't pull too fast. It's got to be like the crab feels the tide pulling him, or he'll let go," he explained, Brian hearing the words he'd spoken last summer echoing now out of his son's mouth, his son's mind like the claws of that crab holding stubbornly onto the bait, not letting any tidbit go, ever, not the word suck nor the name of every character in the Chronicles of Narnia, nor the nationality the word torturer had become tied to on news segments only heard peripherally, but leached into the air. His eye caught a flickering shadow just under the dazzle of light on the water and just then Tim's net darted down and in and came up heavy and twitching with a crab. Tim held it up in front of Yossi's face, then flipped it into the empty white paint can. The crab scuttled on the bottom, its claws raised at them.

"It's very ugly," Yossi said. "Like a, how do you say, *juke*, a cockroach."

"That's gross, Yoss," Tim said.

Brian tapped the pole of the dip net in front of the crab; when it grabbed, Tim reached quickly behind and pulled it up by a back fin. It was a large male, a jimmy, at least six inches between the horns of its shell, the lapis lazuli of its claws startling against the gleaming white underside. He twisted it in front of Yossi. "See, it's a male, Yossi," Tim said. "See the belly—that's the Washington monument. The girls have the Capitol dome on their bellies."

"Go ahead and pull up the pot," Brian said. "Yossi, you can set out a few more lines."

The crab pot dripped with jellyfish when Tim hauled it out of the water, the shapes in it scuttling frantically as the wire cage came into the air, then settling down when it touched the dock, as if a curiosity about their fate had stilled the crabs. It was the same each time. Brian realized he was thinking of them as if they were like the personified creatures from one of the books he read with Tim at night. "Kill the crab, kill the crab," he heard his son chant. He agitated the cage. The crabs fell into a clicking, carapaced mass in one corner, their mouths bubbling and foaming, two with their claws gripping each other's shell and a cracking sound as the steady pressure broke through one, the two crabs staying motionless, locked together and killing each other with the pressure of fear as they waited to be killed. "Kill the crab, kill the crab," Tim sang, and Brian saw, his heart sinking, a shell that wasn't a crab, its top too faceted and symmetrical. He took the pot from Tim, released the stretched rubber tie holding the top edges together and shook the crabs out into the bucket. The empty shell he'd spotted started to fall and he turned the edge away and let it drop onto the dock, along with one crab. The crab, a small one, scurried backwards toward the water, its claws raised at them. It fell in with a plop. "Look at this, Tim," he said, picking up the shell.

It was the nearly emptied, beautifully patterned shell of a diamond-back terrapin. The turtle must have crawled into, or been pulled into, the pot. There were a few tendons of meat webbing the inside of the shell, but otherwise it had been picked clean by the crabs. In the summer, they'd see the turtles all over and sometimes in the car Tim would yell, "Turtle patrol," and Brian would stop on the shoulder of the road and dash out into the highway to pick up one of the doofus, lumbering creatures usually frozen in fear by the noise of the traffic, its head and legs pulled inside. What place did crabs have in the turtles' mythology? What place did crabs have—some turtle horror movie he now saw playing in Tim's glittering eyes as his son fingered the torn meat inside the shell, summarized it in a whispered *wow*: that fascination with gory forms of death that Tim and all his friends had; this male thing Sara didn't understand of dying for, killing for, stamped now on his son's face, Tim already clamoring to be allowed to see movies about Jason and Freddy, the psychopathic, relentlessly mindless murderers who stalked dreams, pressuring to rent *Platoon*; his friends all saw these films, why couldn't he? "Kill the crab, kill the crab," Tim chanted, Yossi smiling and joining in with him.

"Revenge for the turtle," Tim shouted, and Brian thought how he'd taught him to dispatch crabs painlessly before steaming them; you flipped them over, pressed the point of a knife into the top of the tab, the Washington monument or Capitol dome on their bellies, into their hearts. The restaurants did it sometimes to prevent the crabs from losing their claws during steaming; Brian did it because he couldn't stand their frantic clicking under the steamer lid, the thought of their pain. Tim did it because he thought it was neat, asking eagerly to be allowed to stab the crabs, the death fascination a curse of viciousness in his son that scared Brian into pomposity so that he'd delivered a stiff, off-putting lecture about killing only to eat. Yet sometimes Tim was tender, he told himself; turtle patroller, rescuer of a hurt cat from teasing boys.

"Kill the crab, kill the crab," Yossi and Tim sang together, his son's face glowing with happiness and release.

He picked up the bucket and emptied the crabs into the holding cage floating next to the dock. He pulled in the trot lines, too hard, the tightness on one slackening as he jerked it.

"Come on," he said. "Let's get back."

"Aren't we going to take these?" Tim said, disappointed.

"Yossi won't eat them anyway. Would you, Yossi?"

His cousin made a face. "They're disgusting."

They walked back silently through the meadow. The meadow was anything but silent; it hummed and buzzed and whined in Brian's ears, shrill with the noise of insects, billions in one field, hunting, preying on each other, locked in combat. Yossi stuck out his foot and tripped Tim and Tim fell, too heavily. He looked up, dazed, at Yossi, then laughed and jumped at him. Yossi caught him and flipped him upside down. "You rat," Tim yelled. He got up. As he ran toward Yossi, Brian stuck out his foot and Tim fell again. "Yossi and Yossi—two jerks," he said, his voice going a little shrill. Brian pulled him up, then turned his hip into Tim's chest and yanked down on one arm, grabbed him under the armpit and flipped him, a movement still automatic in his muscles after all these years, executed easily on the light body of a child. "Kill the kid, kill the kid," he sang. "You rat, Dad," Tim yelled and Brian flipped him again, Tim falling heavily and up and charging, not laughing now, and Brian put him down again, watching his son's body fall hard into the bushes and he picked him up and slammed him again. Now when Tim's face came up, scratched from the brush, he saw there were tears streaked on his cheeks and Brian understood, his heart falling with a sickening weight, he understood the danger he feared, dug himself in against, uncovered over and over in the earth. He caught Yossi's eye and saw his own panic understood and reflected, Yossi and Yossi, both of them named for a man whose right hand had withered, whose arm had frozen in response to its capacity for violence.

"You hurt me," Tim yelled.

He picked Tim up and tried to hold his squirming body, patted his legs and back. "It was an accident. Where's it hurt?"

Tim jerked away. He was still crying.

"Get away. Soft nuts. Daddy dumb." He kicked at Brian. Brian held him tighter.

"It was an accident, buddy."

"No it wasn't. Let me go, you dork, you abuser. You don't treat me right."

Yossi was staring at them, his face blank and passive, his mouth slightly agape. Brian stroked Tim's hair. "I wouldn't hurt you, buddy, not for the world; you know that. I wouldn't let anything hurt you."

"You hurt me."

Brian looked at Yossi. His Israeli cousin was staring at him silently and then Tim, sobbing, relaxed in Brian's arms. They rocked together, holding on to each other in helpless alliance against the buzzing insistence of the field.

OUR FATHERS' WARS

I INTERVIEWED BRIGADIER GENERAL (RET.) DONALD Turner in his office at his funeral home, just before the town square ceremony during which a new plaque to the dead of the present wars was dedicated—a roll call etched in bronze that served to entomb my friend Dennis into the abstractions of history. Turner had been the force behind the fundraising drive for that plaque, and for the town square war memorial itself. To his credit, he had asked that his contributions, in both effort expended and money donated, be kept anonymous, though he must have known I would be mentioning his connection to the memorial in my article. In any case, Turner had insisted that the interview center on the reasons for his bid to become a County Commissioner, an office that had opened up after Turner had buried Hiram Jasper, the oldest Commissioner and a Democrat. The General was the Republican candidate. My first question had been the standard why-do-you-want-to-run?

"Well," Turner said, chuckling, "I thought of running for county coroner; I've been one way or another in the death business for so long, it seemed a natural move. But to my distress, I found that was an appointed office." His laugh rang slightly false to me, the line clearly a joke he was used to telling. It was a bad time for it. I wasn't in the mood for death jokes. And that little spin had seemed based on the assumption I'd do a fluff piece.

"I wonder if we can get past that kind of good old boy aphorism. Your opponent is contending that you being in what you call the death business in fact doesn't demonstrate any qualifications for the office for which you're running."

Turner cocked his head quizzically, his eyes suddenly glinting, the chuckle frozen into a half-smile.

"Ah," he said.

"Excuse me?"

"All this time we're talking? I've been waiting to see what my daughter told me about you." He held up his hand, as if to stop a question. "Ashley mentioned that you liked to let people lower their expectations, their guard, and then strike." He dropped the hand swiftly, smacked his desk.

It was a large, teak desk, bare except for a leather, gold-embossed date book, a pen holder made from a polished .50 caliber round and a flag set: American, Maryland, and the county. I leaned forward. I was sitting in a straight-backed chair that seemed somehow tilted so that I had to keep pressing my feet against the polished parquet floor to keep from falling off. That sense of being slightly askew somehow fit the place: the office, paneled in dark oak, the built-in shelves on both walls filled with the kind of books furniture stores bought by the pound to use in their floor displays, seemed a displayed idea of itself. As did the General himself, sitting behind his desk: tall, upright, close-shaven; the iron gray hair on both sides of his head still cropped in a military haircut, his nails clipped and buffed, his black, pin-striped suit immaculate, Windsor-knotted tie perfectly square, looking like a depiction of himself, in the way, I couldn't help thinking, one of the corpses he would prepare in this place would look like a representation of the real man.

"I thought it was a fair question."

"General," the General said. "Please."

"General . . ."

"'Good old boy aphorism.'" His smile spread. "What you're accusing me of, is putting on the redneck. Is that right?"

"Are you?"

The smile hadn't moved to his eyes.

"Truth is, Art Sanders, the former owner of this business back in '80, was the friend of an old military comrade who first invited me down to the county. I liked the place; lots of retired military here, the water, the, oh, bucolic scenery," he winked at me, "though that's changing to the worse, isn't it? Ashley tells me you're in some sort of anti-development organization?"

"There's nothing organized about it."

He chuckled, more than the line, my standard comeback, deserved. I waited, my silence also a standard comeback when an interviewee deflected a question.

"Well, part of my decision to come here was because of the county's rapid development," the General said. "To be honest, though you'll find I probably agree with most of your views. I thought, I suppose, to have the best of both worlds: an area only a few hours from the city, still pretty and agricultural, but growing, money to be made. My friend showed me the books, talked about the rising population in the county, gave me a good price. I've done well here. I want to give back."

"I see."

His eyes narrowed. "But you don't believe me."

"I didn't say that."

"It's how you are coming across, son. Hunter—may I call you that—I understand that today is a particularly stressful day for you. My deepest sympathies. I plan to say a few words at the ceremony."

"Well, that will be appropriate."

"At least your friend will be properly honored. That did not happen in my war, nor to folks such as your father. Ashley told me what your dad had to deal with before he made the choice to take his own life. I fault no man for that. They are all casualties of war to me. And they are all still my brothers-in-arms."

My still brothers were the words that settled into my mind. I didn't say anything.

"I understand your dad, and I understand you have lost a friend, and how you must feel today, son. But there is something I want you to understand." He gestured around the parlor. "About who I am." He got up from behind the large desk and walked to the window, shadows from the blinds striping his face. "This profession was my father's profession, Mr. Reed. Growing up, I was the brunt of jokes—boys and sometimes girls, in the high school developed a habit of pinching their nostrils when I went by, as if I stunk of corpses. But my father was one of the kindest men I knew, and he helped many families deal with their grief. Taking up this profession was a way I tried to get back to his . . . kindness. It was why I became a medic."

His voice was nearly a whisper now. I had started to like him.

I waited for the General to continue, but the man was suddenly silent, looking at me expectantly. What was expected from the reference to Vietnam, I supposed, was "thank you for your service," a phrase I no longer used since hearing Dennis, back between deployments and seeing those words on a banner at Jiffy Lube, had inquired about the number of corpses that had to be produced in order to be thanked for each itemized task: one corpse for an oil change, two for tire rotation, and so on. The attendant hadn't gotten it. It's a courtesy, sir, he'd said. Thank you for your service.

Brigadier General Donald Turner's service, as described on the campaign literature he suddenly handed to me with an aggressive rustle, had begun as a teenage medic in a Special Forces "A" team during the early, advisory, days of the Vietnam War; he had been decorated with the Silver Star for bravery, putting his own body between men he was working on and the enemy. After his discharge, he had gone for a degree in Mortuary Science—his father's profession—at Northwestern, and then had come back into the service after OCS, as an officer, serving not in his funerary capacity but as a combat infantry commander. He survived two more tours in Vietnam, coming out as a colonel; he was promoted to Brigadier General upon his retirement. Afterwards—the timeline I had was somewhat hazy about this part of Turner's life—he had taken over his family's funeral business in Bethesda for a number of years before selling it and coming to the county.

I had read all this before, the material emailed to me prior to the interview. I looked now from the pages, to the General, and then back to the paper. The General reduced to his essence. There I am. *There it is,* my father would say. Turner's life after his military service was for the most part AWOL from that sheet, even though it had contained a wife who died in childbirth, and the child of that sacrifice, now come into my own heart. I wondered at that absence, what the choice to omit said about Turner. I started to formulate a question, but as the General looked at me, leaning forward slightly in expectation, it died in my mouth. In its place I threw him a softball, asking why he had chosen to go back into the Army as an infantry officer after college.

"I was S.O. G. Special Operations Groups," the General corrected. "There's a difference."

"I apologize. But . . ."

"It's not important. What I am saying is that I see my profession as a way I still serve. I see becoming a commissioner in the same light. I want to be of service, son. I am not accustomed to being a private citizen."

He put his elbows on his desk and brought his hands together as if in prayer, staring at me over the peak of them. "I always felt I had abandoned the dead," he said. "Failed them. Both as a medic and later as a commanding officer. I never made bad errors of judgment; I always tried to accomplish missions with the least amount of casualties. But still. Your father was a soldier. He would have understood me."

"Yes. He might have."

Turner looked up, held my gaze. "Each time I conducted a funeral, brought any comfort to a family's grief, it was, it is, as if I were burying one of my soldiers. Can you understand that, son?"

I nodded. The General of the Dead, I thought.

• • •

After our interview I had walked from Turner's Funeral Home to the Leonardtown town square. Walked in my mind with Dennis. My friend's death anniversary was now wrapped into the larger mourning of Memorial Day, though there was not very much grieving in evidence. People were already gathering for the dedication ceremony; my own grief, thick in my chest and throat and somehow swollen further by the General's words, separated me from them, as if I were behind a glass wall that stood between myself and the crowd of spectators waving small American flags, buying ice cream and funnel cakes, noisy with a holiday exuberance that seemed more about dissipating the dead than commemorating them.

A large plywood platform, hung with swags of red, white and blue bunting, and rows of folding chairs had been set up for the dignitaries and guests. The new addition to the memorial was draped with gray cloth, a small, Druidic altar in front of the concrete slab into which were set the three brass plates engraved with the names of KIAs from World War Two, Korea and Vietnam. There were thirteen names on the latter, the number of men, my father had muttered when that memorial had first been unveiled, in a Marine rifle squad. Not much for a war, he'd say. Unless it was a war that wasn't worth a hair on the ass of one of those thirteen.

Three tall flagpoles stood above the names, the county, state and national flags flapping, their ropes and grommets clanging against the aluminum. The square could have been some Hollywood conception of what a small Southern town should look like. But I liked it. Its renovation had been part of an effort by the county to keep the kind of downtown center that some years ago had seemed on the verge of extinction, done in by malls that themselves would soon be done in by the internet. The grassed square that held the memorials, as well as benches and flowerbeds filled with red geraniums, was bordered by four streets lined by old brick or clapboard buildings, now mostly occupied by local eateries. A small French restaurant now held what had been Earl's bar and lunch counter (the Duke of Earl's members of my father's generation always called it, a reference I didn't get for years). The crumbling brick building still had Earl's sole advertisement painted on its second story: EAT, though its other marker, *Whites Only*, existed only in how-far-we've-come anecdotes. The county courthouse sat a block away, a brick building with a portico entrance fronted by white pillars. Next to it was an old, gray slate jail house, now owned by the historical society. A black cannon lay on the grass nearby, and next to it, a stone surrounded by a small picket fence, with no marker next to it: locals knew it as the Witch's Stone, after an old lady whose bad disposition was thought to bring disastrous storms. She had been chased out of her home and into a blizzard by an angry mob, sometime in the eighteenth century. When they found her body, she was clutching the stone. There were people who, looking at it, supposedly could see her handprints sunk into the rock. I was not one of them.

It was true, I did like the town center, though looking at it now it struck me the same way Turner's office had: an idea of itself, slightly hedged from reality. The idea of an ideal. What that ideal was originally—or rather, one's nostalgia for it—didn't bear too close an inspection. At one time this place had been the location of the auction block for slave sales: it was up the street—Washington Street—from a dock where slave ships landed, and the long, sad coffles had shuffled up the steep hill to the square, their ankles bleeding from the chafing of the shackles, their eyes squinting in the strange North American light that pierced them like needles after the dark confinement of the Middle Passage. The blood trails were invisible now, under the cobblestones and concrete, but the trace of their legacy remained on the World War One memorial at the east end of the square. It was a standard war monument, a simple stone block with the names of the dead listed on brass plaques, but when you looked closely, you could see that, unlike Earl's, the names were still divided under the labels "White" and "Colored," even the commemorated dead segregated.

I was looking at the names when I heard Ashley's voice behind me. "Are they ever going to change that?"

"I don't think they should. It's kind of a memorial to two things."

"Bullshit," she said, and put her arms around my waist. "You OK?"
I turned and kissed her.

"No," I said.

"Nor should you be."

Ashley Turner had her father's lanky height, straight corn-blonde hair that she wore down to her ass, and a kind of deceptive fragility that made her strength of character, when you got to know her, somehow more impressive. Her bones, under her pale skin, always looked brittle to me, though I knew she had been a lacrosse player in college and had never even twisted an ankle. I held her tightly, pushing her into the hollows her question had opened in me.

"How did it go with Daddy?"

"Not too badly."

"He have you in the Rickover chair?"

"Excuse me?"

"Black walnut? Straight-backed? You find yourself somewhat uncomfortable? "

"Are you kidding me?"

"The chair was something he got from reading a book by Admiral Rickover. Shorten the front legs a little, keep the person distracted, under pressure."

She shook her head. "Dear old daddy."

"Jesus."

"No," she said. "Just dear old daddy. There he is." She pointed with her chin, as her father, the General of the Dead, took his place on the platform. Then she turned to me.

"I'm so sorry, Hunter."

Her words opened again whatever I'd been trying to clench inside and my eyes filled. A discordant bray of trumpets and trombones sounded from down the street. Various dignitaries were mounting the speakers' podium: county commissioners, members of the school board, a senator, and so on. I dutifully checked them off in my notebook.

Ashley slipped an arm around my waist as if afraid I would float away. Someone clashed two cymbals together. It was such a nice town. A child laughed in delight. I closed my eyes for a second. When I opened them, George Groves, the director of the new VA Center, was looking at me, over the side of the platform. Groves was a large man, still as fit as when he became the first black athlete from the county to get a full scholarship to Morgan State. He was a Vietnam veteran too, had done three tours, was awarded a Distinguished Service Cross for rallying and saving his entire company when they'd been ambushed by a North Vietnamese regiment. He'd been a captain at the time, had retired as a colonel, and was one of the few officers my father ever respected. Groves was from one of the oldest African American families in the county: his ancestors had been freed by George Washington for service in the Revolution and owned large tracts of land in the 7th District, along the Potomac. Two later ancestors were on the World War One monument, in the Colored section. When Groves was growing up, he would not have been able to eat at Earl's, and if a white man had walked towards him, down the sidewalk along this square, he'd have known to step out of the way and get down into the gutter. It was a time that seemed as thankfully distant to me as the slave auctions once held in this place, even though I knew it had happened, right here where I stood with the daughter of the General of the Dead.

Himself, in a black pin-striped suit, white tie and shirt, the small rectangular metal pin representing his Silver Star on his lapel, had followed Groves's gaze over the edge of the stand and saw us. He winked, and pantomimed scribbling in an imaginary notebook. I nodded up to him.

The crowd began cheering. The parade began. The high school marching band. The Paintball Club, a somewhat para-military group of teenagers who liked to dress in camouflage and shoot each other in the woods. They were led by Paul Rausch, who did what was euphemistically called a "news" talk show, on local radio.

The firefighters came next, and Fish and Game—some boos from the crowd—and then the Sheriff's Department, in their Smokey the

Bear hats. Russell Hallam, the county sheriff, was also on the speakers' platform, and I thought briefly about doing an article about the change in racial attitudes in the county, with both a black administrator and a black sheriff. The New South. But I knew I was just trying to distract myself; everything I looked at gathered around Dennis and my dad.

It struck me again how many veterans there were in this place. Small town America. Hallam was a Vietnam vet too. And Turner. And Rausch. They weren't sitting together, but in my mind they formed a little knot, set apart. They all knew each other, and they all had known my father and Emmett Wheeler, Dennis's father. Growing up, it had seemed to me and Dennis that they, the veterans, were an exclusive club that spoke in its own secret code, communicated volumes of experience with covert glances, with chuckles and jokes and sudden silences, initiates of a select warrior clan. They had been seared and sanctified and their war, the real war—not the abstraction of it such as this ceremony was—had been shut away in dark attics like the family secret, the crazy cousin kept shackled and filthy and far away, kept long of tooth and nail and howling behind the locked door in the place you couldn't go or ask about. Their war was like the forbidden country of sex, held, as if in sealed boxes, in the combat video games my friends all played but that were not allowed in my house, the war movies I was not allowed to see, so that when I snuck home the tapes, and later, the DVDs or downloads, I could only watch them alone, in secret, feeling as I did a shift under the heart, a tightening in the testicles.

Now the rest of the club was marching to the square, led by another vet, Stuart Winters, a barrel-chested World War II paratrooper who always organized the parade and yelled at his scraggly, middle-aged troops as if he were still the sergeant major he'd once been.

If my father was still alive, he would not have marched here today. He hated parades.

The veterans took their places in the first two rows of folding chairs in front of the stand. A smaller row, three seats, had been set up in front of them. The chairs were still empty. I stared at them. The final group marched down the street, filed onto the square: an honor guard, at platoon strength, from the local National Guard unit. They were wearing pressed desert fatigues, their boots sand-brown, and most of them had the Combat Infantry Badge with its the musket against a blue background, pinned on their chests. They had just returned from their Iraq deployment the month before and were scheduled to redeploy on June 13. A swell of applause and cheers followed their march.

"And so they get their parade," Ashley said.

She glanced at me out of the corner of her eye. I didn't reply, didn't feel like taking up the gauntlet she had thrown.

"I'm sorry," she said again.

The National Guard troopers placed the flags in their tripods, and then stood at attention and saluted.

The band began playing the Marines' hymn and the crowd on the north side of the square began applauding, a wave of it following a white Cadillac moving slowly up Washington Street. I saw Jackson Millicent, the fire chief, dressed in a seersucker suit with a paisley tie, behind the wheel, but I couldn't make out his back seat passenger until he pulled up next to the dignitaries' stand. Millicent stopped the car, got out, went around, opened the other door, and extended his arm. Dennis's mother took it, placing her hand on his forearm, and rose from the door. Xuân Wheeler looked fragile and old, her hair uncombed: a different woman than the one I had always felt guilty about seeing, my best friend's mother, as exotic and strikingly attractive. She was wearing a black Vietnamese outfit—a high-collared silk tunic slit at the hips, over trousers. I remembered how at Dennis's funeral she had laid a white band on his coffin. It was the kind of band that Vietnamese wrapped around their heads at funerals for parents, Dennis had once told me, though I suppose it was different when the parent was burying the child. Emmett Wheeler, Dennis's father, was not with his wife. Later, I found out that he had refused to come. The crowd went silent for a moment, except for some kids, running in circles spinning sparklers and laughing. But it was only a brief pause. In another moment, the adults were chattering again also. I hated them.

Only the National Guard remained silent. They had come to attention. And gave Xuân Wheeler a slow hand salute, raising their arms and bringing the blades of their hands to their foreheads in exact unison.

The band began to play the anthem, and people sung along, hands on hearts. When the speeches began, I started, out of habit, to take notes in my reporter's notebook. There was no need. It was the expected string of clichés, uttered as if they were freshly discovered wisdom. But not something at which I felt the need to sneer. The occasion was far removed from what my father would call the blood and shit. But for a moment it held me where I needed to be, and such distracting myths that were solemnly pronounced in this place were as much a part of what centered the town and myself as this square, with its flowers and benches and memorials, the spoken and unspoken histories that bound us.

Xuân Wheeler sat stiffly throughout the speeches, her lips tightened, as if concentrating all her strength on keeping her body from physically flying into pieces. Emmett should have been with her. But I wasn't surprised at his absence. Dennis's father was enough like my own for me to know how he would hate all this. At Dennis's funeral, he'd gotten up and walked away when the Marine honor guard tried to give him the folded American flag. Xuân took it. Dennis's sister, Tuyết, was at Boston University; she had come for the funeral, and I knew her well enough also to understand how she would feel about this, how she would hate to see her brother's name trapped here.

Three sixth graders were invited up to read their Memorial Day poems. The General of the Dead rose and reminded the crowd that freedom wasn't free and of their eternal gratitude to those who had sacrificed to give them that freedom. His words finally broke the spell. I could no longer bear it. What was the freedom that Dennis gifted to these people, with his dirty death in a devastated city that hated his presence, that saw his very life as somehow offensive? In the present situation in which we find ourselves, the General said from the podium. The General would go far. He already had the politician's skill, not that different from a mortician's, of making death attractive. Maybe that was the answer to his questions about his qualifications for office. Ashley was looking at me, her cool hand tightening on my arm. Had I spoken out loud? The General and George Groves stepped down from the platform, and both saluted Mrs. Wheeler, and I felt her fragility like a brittleness in his own bones. My friend's mother. I focused on the names of the dead from three wars, on the panel from the Vietnam War, with its thirteen names, county names, and I thought again about the name that wasn't on it but should be, my father killed finally by that war he had brought home and given to me as an unwanted legacy, a definition that pressed in on me like the bamboo slats of a prisoner's narrow cage. The way Emmett Wheeler's Vietnam had pressed in on Dennis, as if he were born to receive his father's postponed death.

Turner picked up the cord that, when pulled, would reveal the new dead to be added onto those rows.

"Burnt offerings," Ashley muttered.

Her father handed the cord to Xuân Wheeler. Or tried to. She kept her hands folded in her lap, her lips tight. A low mutter rippled through the crowd. The General nodded and smiled gently at her, his face suffused with sympathy. He pulled the cord. The cloth fell away, revealing the new plaque. War Against Terror. The words struck me, not for the first time, as something from science fiction. Terra versus Terror. Why not the war against panic? The war against nightmares?

There were three names on the small plaque and the second name was Dennis Thọ Wheeler. The sight of his middle name stabbed me, the irrational thought coming to me that it was its exposure that had killed him. The revelation of his secret name. I turned away and looked at Xuân, at my friend's mother who had been born and lived through and then fled her own war in the fragility of a small boat on an open sea, who had lost a country and had come to this place, light as a ghost, to rebuild that stolen life. Whose child in that stolen life had died in the terrible noise that had been the soundtrack of her first life, in some foul canal that ran through the wasteland of an alien city, a place so different than the green of her first and second countries. Wasted in a wasteland. I looked at the names again. I didn't know the other two well—Roger Gulland and Thomas Hewitt—one my age, twenty-nine, the other only nineteen. A lot from a small town, but it was the small towns that were providing the bodies for this war: the kids who enlisted because it was a way out or a way to get a job or a way to get money for college or a way to get some excitement or as a rite of passage or because the town needed something to do on Memorial Day or because they envisioned themselves standing with their initiated elders on that platform, the generals of the dead. It was what you did.

Turner saluted the plaque, and then bent and whispered into Xuân Wheeler's ear. He passed her the microphone. She stared at it. The silence was only broken by a baby's wail. She brought the microphone to her lips.

"Too much," she said. Her lips were too close to the microphone, and the words trained into a loud, electronic screech. From someplace, a child laughed.

"Too much," she said again. The smile was pasted on Turner's face. Next to me, Ashley was weeping, her shoulders heaving.

"Too much," she said again, and Turner smiled and nodded at her, like the funeral director he was, and tried to take back the mike. She snatched it to her breast, rose.

"Too much," she screamed into it. The people on the stand were looking at each other, the crowd muttering. The mayor mouthed something to Turner. I heard a groan, and looked over at the ranks of the National Guardsmen. Several of them had tears streaming down their faces. Then two of the soldiers broke ranks and ignored the barked orders of their sergeants and did what I knew I should have done, ran over to Mrs. Wheeler and threw their arms around her, and she rested her face against the chest of one boy and I could see his shoulders moving up and down as he sobbed. But then, over the boy's shoulder, she saw the name on the stone and she screamed, a wordless scream this time, and she thrust herself past the boy and got down on her knees and tried to rub out the name Thọ, rub out her son's secret name, his death name, with bleeding fingers.

• • •

I'd wanted to see her after the ceremony, but she was put into the back of the Cadillac and whisked away, hustled off like an embarrassment. I stared after her, breathing heavily, my chest and throat tight with rage. After a few seconds I became aware that Ashley was stroking my arm.

"Let's walk," she said.

We pushed through the crowd, or rather the crowd funneled us, towards the courthouse. Ashley took my hand. We went by the cannon in front of the old jailhouse and then stopped at the Witch's Rock. Ashley bent and touched it, a quick brush of her fingers. When Dennis, Tuyết and I were kids, we would dare each other to sit on it, a dare that no one ever took up. I looked at it, as I always did, searching for the handprints. I still couldn't see them. I tried to see Dennis's name, his first and his secret name, tried to make them appear on the rock. They didn't. It came to me that I was still in the same place I'd been when I was a kid. I had gone nowhere. I still saw with the same eyes. I thought about Tuyết. I knew that what she would hate about her brother's name being engraved on a stone in the town square was that sense that he also had never escaped this place, encapsulated in its own past, its own smug and self-protective insularity, its separate listings of Colored and White that evoked the other chained and unnamed processions that had shuffled under this sun to this place while another crowd prodded and lashed their flesh. Its lies about all its wars repeated until they became holy truth, as if through the chants of a prayer. I had only gotten away for the few years I'd gone to university, in-state at that, and now I was still here, this place pulled around me like a comforter.

"Did you ever notice," I said to Ashley, "that their parents gave Dennis the American name and Tuyết the Vietnamese name and she looked more Vietnamese than him. I mean, how could they know?"

Ashley said nothing.

"When my father was my age, he had already been a sergeant of Marines."

She swiveled around and stared at me. "What are you talking about?"

"Winters sent me papers again. For the Guard. I'm thinking of doing it."

"Are you out of your fucking mind?"

"It's something I need to do."

"Something you need to do? Jesus, Hunter, did you just say that? You don't even believe in the fucking war."

"There are things I owe."

"I don't even know you when you talk in platitudes like that. It's like someone is speaking through your mouth." She squatted down, put her hand on the rock, splaying out her fingers.

"I could never see it," I said. "The handprint."

"Shit, give me your hand." She yanked it down. She was very angry. She pressed my hand against the stone. "There. Can you feel it?"

"No."

She was right. I was an informed person. I knew about the manipulation of intelligence, the lies fashioned from wishful thinking. All the parallels with my father's war: a false premise of danger to the nation, an enemy interlaced with the civilians you were there to protect and liberate, a corrupt government to prop up. A war in which you went down a road as Dennis Thọ Wheeler had gone down the road, hung out as bait. It didn't matter. I wanted to be a carrier of dark secrets, to own and bring back eyes seared by scenes of unimaginable horror to a place where such scenes were abstracted and removed, extant only on screen. I wanted to be able to stand at attention in the sun and look at the speakers on the platform with an earned contempt and cynicism, a dark knowledge that negated their bombast. I wanted the earned irony of my father's derisive laughter. I wanted all of it, everything except my name on a plaque on the town square, and sometimes I wanted that as well.

I looked over at the National Guardsmen, standing at ease now, joking with each other, handling their weapons casually. I knew that, no matter what he said, if my father were here, he would see his real sons as those soldiers returned from the fire. I thought back to the interview, Ashley's dad telling me how he felt about the dead. Your father was a soldier, he had said. He would have understood.

Ashley was staring at me. "Too much," she said.

SEARCH AND DESTROY

THERE WERE FIERY NEEDLE PRICKS IN HIS FOOT, JABS felt through a half dream, and he kicked out. His foot connected with something warm and hairy, and he sat up abruptly, sleep sucked away from him like water down a drain. "Shit," he said.

He lived in a hootch at Marble Mountain Air Facility with ten others. They had a parachute hung under the ceiling and partitions and shelves made of scrap wood and straw matting. Home-made, home-making.

Up to the month before, the hootch had been a canvas-roofed tent and almost unbearably hot. The new tin roof made it much cooler inside. "But now we got rats in here," he said to Rodriguez.

"Yes, indeedy," said Rodriguez. "And it seems it's been raining more since you white men invented this tin stuff."

"Rats," Sam said, shaking his head. He was lying on his cot, reading a paperback. "Jesus Christ. Rats."

"Don't let it worry you," Torenelli said.

Eventually it worried all of them.

At least once a night someone would be snapped awake by the feel of a small hot body somewhere in his cot. Usually the rats preferred to attack feet, two naked hunks of meat that tended to become exposed in the night. Sam, for one, could never get back to sleep after feeling a rat. He would begin to drop off, then a mental picture of the animal eating his nose or an eye, jumping across the floor with a chunk of Sam-face dangling from its mouth, would wake him up. He began to sleep hunched protectively over his genitals, like a man about to fight.

There was a constant squealing at night. It got on the men's nerves, and they would lie awake listening, feeling the sweat from their backs wetting the sandy canvas of their cots. Often they could see the small dimples the rats' feet made as they ran along the top side of the hanging parachute. The men would throw things at the impressions, but the rats were too fast.

It wasn't until Torenelli was killed that it became an obsession to kill the rats. The night before it happened, he had flipped out at the soft scuffling noises on the silk above his head, and had shot a few holes in the roof with his .45. He would have been court-martialed if he hadn't caught a .50 round that blew most of his chest away, on a medevac the next day.

The rats became a jinx to the men on flight pay after that. They began calling them gooks.

They would lie awake at night, waiting. When someone would feel or hear a rat, he'd yell gook! and Perez would switch on the light. They would chase the creature frantically, upsetting cots, tripping over sea-bags. It would have been a funny Keystone Kops scene, except for the hate and fear in the Marines' eyes.

At the weekly movie, shown outdoors on a sheet tacked onto a wall of sandbags, they didn't laugh anymore at the little cartoon mice. They would stare at them with hate-rimmed, sleepless eyes and look at the people who did laugh as though they were idiots.

Perez almost got one once. He was chasing it with a Montagnard spear he had picked up near Khe Sanh. He cornered the rat and was trying to jab it with the spear, mock-dueling, laughing hysterically. The animal suddenly reared up on its hind legs and drew back its thin rubber lips, exposing sharp, wicked-looking teeth. Its eyes bulged with frantic hate. Perez was taken aback and stopped jabbing for a split second. The rat immediately leapt away and disappeared into some unseen hole.

On the day the hunt was finally successful they killed eleven rats. It happened right after Perez and Billings were knocked out of the air while on a resupply to Hill 327. A recoilless rifle round had punched a huge hole in the side of their helicopter, but they were able to auto-rotate down with no one hurt.

They all sat around that night telling sea stories about getting shot down. Perez was grateful the round hadn't exploded the gas tank. "Thank fuck it didn't explode," he said. All it had meant was a little time with the grunts for his gunner, Billings, and him. He was shaking his head when they all heard the squeal, punctuating his prayer. "Gook!" Perez yelled, his face hard.

The slick brown body jumped across the room, and they flew after it, yelling. They were surprised to trap the rat almost immediately. It stood on its hind legs in an inescapable corner, squealing shrilly.

Sam was the first to see why the rat was so easily trapped. He heard a soft noise from the opposite corner of the hut and went to look. Billings saw him move and followed. "Damn," he yelled, fervently, triumphantly, "it's got babies! It was trying to lead us away."

There were ten of them, blind and pink, clutching at each other with small groping hands. Billings took a long piece of copper wire and, kneeling, stuck its end through each baby's small, pulsing throat. The tinny sound of their squealing gradually died as the wire tore through flesh, until only the squeal of the trapped mother could be heard.

Billings whooped and brandished the chain of dead babies in front of the mother, Then he took them outside and plunged their still twitching mass into the large water barrel just outside the hut. His face was alight and strained.

Donner, the big silent boy from Kansas, clubbed at the mother. She kept up her high-pitched squealing, her eyes darting towards the water barrel outside. Perez grabbed a canvas sack and dropped it over the stunned rat. The rest of the men stood around him, watching. He picked the sack up and carried it outside to the barrel, then took it by the bottom and shook the mother out into the water. The two ends of the wire on which the babies were dangling had caught on the rim of the barrel, and the bodies just broke the water, next to her face. She was still alive, swimming frantically.

Perez began pushing her face under with a piece of wood. He kept holding her down for longer and longer periods, but each time he let up she would still be alive and struggling. He swore at her.

Donner went into the hut and came back with his can of deodorant. He waited until Perez let the rat's head break the water, then sprayed the deodorant through the flame of his cigarette lighter. It sent out a sheet of flame: a miniature flame thrower. The hair on her face began to burn off, leaving her with surprisingly pink skin that soon blackened and began peeling off like singed paper. Her eyes changed from alive black berries to small dead ones and then to cinders. They could almost see her blood boil. She kept coming up alive.

Perez and Donner began to look panicky. "Die, goddamn you," Perez swore, under his breath. The rest of the men watched silently. Both Perez and Donner were sweating profusely. They held the rat under for impossibly long periods, but she kept surfacing, her burned face coming up next to her dead babies, her mouth opening and closing, grabbing lungfuls of air and fire.

After a long time, she died.

Perez and Donner stood there for a while looking at her gently bobbing body. Their mouths were hanging open and they looked drained and exhausted. Everybody else went silently back into the hootch.

MEMORIAL DAYS

I WILL USE THE DAY TO REMEMBER DENNIS.

At the point from which I start to paddle, the channel is only a few yards wide and the water shallow and brown over a bottom of mud, pebbles, matted leaves and branches. Some of the branches scrape like fingernails along the kayak's bottom and an escort of panicked darters dance over the surface of the water, in front of and alongside me. The banks are tangled with bushes and holly and the branches of the sycamores and elms and oaks arch and interweave overhead. In the shaded spots the water is transparent, and where sunspots filter through the shifting leaves they touch off, like paint dissipating from the tip of a brush, amoebic milky shapes on the surface, and when I shift my eyes off them and take in the surrounding water, swirled with fallen leaves, it turns into a shifting tan and white camouflage.

As the woods close around me, I feel bands of tension I haven't even been aware of loosen from my forehead and chest. The light that breaks through the lace of leaves runs along with me as I paddle, the sparkle awakening as if the brush of my sight on the water created it. When I round a bend I see a blue heron, large as a five-year-old child. Fishing. It looks up, gives an impatient squawk and does its disjointed, mechanical-toy heron takeoff, soaring from awkwardness to grace as it enters its element and wings downstream, following the cambering of the creek and staying low. It is his kingdom, and I call out that I am just a visitor, mean him no harm, something I'd learned from Dennis,

171

picked up from a children's book Dennis had liked, though, even at eight years old a mythmaker, he had first claimed it as local legend.

I am in the country of childhood now, in a child's dream that I could enter through some portal in a tree or in a wardrobe, pass over into the shadowlands. Gliding into the country of memory, coached by the day's memorial purpose. I follow the heron's flight until the night I'd met Ashley and lost Dennis assembles for me, my perception conjugating to an endless flowing present tense; I am again in Bledsoe's Bar and Dennis is telling me he has joined the Marines and I am rigid with an anger that is partly envy and partly an anticipation of the grief I feel now.

How does your father feel about it, I ask him.

Dennis keeps grinning silently, through a wreath of smoke, through the thin curtain of marsh grass, through the scrim of heat-mist rising off the surface of the water. He leans forward, coming out of the mist and the barroom gloom, clarifying. In the strobing neon bar signs sometimes he looks like his Vietnamese mother, an Asian cast to his cheekbones and eyes, his hair black and straight, but he has his father's size, bulk and broad shoulders and sometimes he is taken for a Wesort, usurping the mix that flows in my own family's blood from the run-away Brit indentureds, renegade Piscataways and escaped African slaves who once found refuge together in the Southern Maryland marshes. He doesn't answer my question.

I don't blame him, I say. *He doesn't want you to become him.*

Dennis's grin widens. *What's wrong with my father?*

Same thing was wrong with mine.

Your dad was a better man because of Vietnam. It gave him the guts to check out when he had to.

It gave him the reason to do it. That fucking year in his life pressed like a lid on all the rest of his years.

The creek widens and the dip of the paddle propels me back to the slipping present. I pass further into marshland, the forest opening to acres of undulating cord grass, jeweled with dew-flecked spider webs and picketed here and there with looming hundred-foot sentinels of loblolly pine, some of them standing dead and white and skeletal. The tide line is a little low, exposing the muddied bottoms of the grass stalks. Clusters of small brown snails cling to the stalks and I remember how Dennis once told me that his mother would gather the snails, soak them overnight in rice water to clean them, then steam them with lemon grass, ginger and lime leaves and eat them with fish sauce mixed with sugar, lime juice, finely chopped chili and garlic. The snails were emissaries from her own shadowland of memories, shelled inhabitants of a Mekong she could sometimes transpose over Southern Maryland scenes, coax the water lilies into brilliant lotus blossoms that floated on the billowing green robes of water fairies, rooted in mud and petaling in sun. Whenever Dennis went fishing, he would gather those snails for her, though when we were kids, he made me promise not to tell any of our classmates. It was one of the secrets that knit us, that existed to knit us, like our fantasy of the shadowlands, and Dennis's middle, Vietnamese, name that no one else could know.

Tough to be the children of myths, I say to Dennis.

Tough titty. The only way, my friend, to escape the legend, is to make your own legend.

The marsh stretches around me, the fetid smell of it thickening in my nostrils whenever my paddle brings up gobs of mud. I round a bend, paddle away from the tendrils of memories, my father's stories of his war floating into my memories of Dennis's mother, Xuân, and the secret name Dennis told me must never be pronounced, or a ghost would drown him. This marsh had been our Vietnam when we were kids, trying to be our fathers, humping the wetlands with plastic rifles and later BB guns, enduring the heat and insect bites. Though Dennis, more often than not, played being Viet Cong, his father's old enemies. I like winners, he said to me. The games we played, waiting impatiently for the chance to bring the real thing into our lives. I miss him, and I miss my father and the country I float through once again diffuses and transforms in the heat haze into that country whose name was never uttered except as the name of a war or the name of a curse. Vietnam-the-war drawn like a gauze veil over everything I—and Dennis and his sister Tuyết and Ashley—saw, as if that were our inheritance.

I can no longer see bottom, only a ghost crest of wavering grass beneath the surface of the creek.

I dig the paddle in, left and right, finding a rhythm, the motion rocking me to another memory of my father: Jack had sneered at the kayak, called it a yuppie toy. The S.S. *Minnow*. You've gone over to the enemy, boy. I shut my eyes, my skim over the water the glide my father had taken into another country where I couldn't follow. No more than I could follow Dennis's Humvee as it rose impossibly on an expanding bubble of gas and flame and tipped into a scum-rimed, garbage-clogged canal running alongside a street in some shithole town in Anbar Province: my friend from this estuarine place where we had both grown up, drowning, as if a ghost had found his secret name. Drowning in that trash-filled, reed-choked alien water now somehow confluent to the creek upon which I have now come to commemorate him on this Memorial Day.

I paddle harder, racing against ghosts. In Bledsoe's Bar it is the night I lost Dennis to the war and found Ashley. She turns and looks at me from across the marsh grass, from across the space between our tables in the barroom gloom, a slim, blonde woman whose eyes flit past mine and then back and then don't look away. Her eyes are gray and full of intelligence, her face shadowed and then lit by the sputter of a neon Old Boh sign on the wall behind the bar. She licks nervously at the beer foam on her lips and a little frisson run through my veins, a jolt of recognition that for a time afterwards I will like to think of as a premonition, our future together folding back in time to touch and inform that moment. Though what I understand now is it was our fathers' war that linked us. The same unrequested history that tied me to Dennis. Filtered that night through the war waiting for Dennis. She smiles at me. I think I see her nod slightly, as if approving my words. My anger at Dennis for going to the war. Dennis catches my stare. Sees what I see in it. Winks at Ruth, his girl that night, and then grins, swivels towards Ashley.

Darlene, I'd like you to meet my good friend Hunter.

My name's not Darlene.

Well, hell, I'm half right.

She stares at him. I can see her trying to repress a smile; Dennis's inevitable effect. *Why on earth are you going into the Marines,* she asks him, then flushes. *I'm sorry. I wasn't eavesdropping.*

Dennis grins again, pats the empty chair next to mine.

Sure you were. Come on over. You kids were made for each other.

She smiles at me.

Is that right?

I hope so, I say, with no humor at all. She blinks quickly, a stalker-warning flickering in her eyes, and I smile, trying to silently reassure her that I am sane.

Come on over, Dennis says again.

You may not like what I have to say.

Hell, you already threw the chum in the water, honey.

He pats the seat next to me again.

Come over, sit on down. Speak your mind.

She hesitates a moment and then gives a what-the-hell shrug, rises, picks up her beer, joins us.

The question is, she says, *whether or not you really believe in the war.*

He will if he has to, I say.

Hey, I'm proud of him, we're fighting fanatics, Ruth says.

You know what the aim of fanaticism is, Ashley says.

My aim is fine, Dennis says. *Best thing about me.*

At least nobody's going to spit on him when he comes back, Ruth says.

I support the soldiers. Anyway, that's such an urban myth, Ashley says.

I had an uncle, Ruth says.

I have a father, Ashley says.

Support the troops, Dennis says, grinning wickedly. *Whoop, whoop, whoop. Support the troops. That's the trick. With stickers and bumpers and ribbons, oh my.*

He and Ruth begin to sing it.

Stickers and bumpers and ribbons, oh my.
Stickers and bumpers and ribbons, oh my.
Stickers and bumpers and ribbons, oh my.

Bullshit, Ashley says. She glares at me. *I support them by wanting to get them home safe.*

Sure thing, I say. I would have said anything to keep her next to me. To have her back. To have him back. I am mourning both of them. I'm in a fucking swamp mourning two losses. Though the distance between Ashley and me is only the distance of failed love and fading time. She is still alive, exists somewhere beyond the cage of my memories; Dennis is only the mist pierced like a tattered white curtain by the reeds around me.

Still, I lost them both to the war.

Your name is Hunter? Well, isn't that reassuring.

It's an old county name, I say defensively, and then think of another. *At least it's not Minor.*

Beer explodes from Dennis's nostrils. *Minor Dobson. 7th Grade. What a tool.*

Ashley giggles. *Minor? As in Major?*

That's right. Anyway what kind of name is Ashley? Lady Ashley? Your parents into Hemingway?

Fucking Hunter, Dennis says. *Like everyone in the world gets his references. Like anybody reads books.*

My father, Ashley says primly, *is a funeral director.*

Oh shit, Dennis says. *The General. I heard of him.* He salutes her.

Least I don't want to be a Hemingway character, Den, I say.

A flat-bottomed wooden skiff is anchored among the cord grass in a small side stream that is hidden by the reeds until I am almost up on it. An Amish girl, in her bonnet and homespun cotton dress, is standing in the bow, fishing with a bamboo pole; at the stern a straw-hatted, beardless boy sits baiting a hook. They could be brother and sister. Both are motionless; they fasten me into a silent past I want to keep wrapped around myself. As if complicit in the need, they ignore me. I am an impossible intrusion from a future century, an awkward slip in time. Seeing myself through their eyes. Through my Wesort eyes, my father would have said, calling up the occasional shifts in sight descendants of that blood mix supposedly experienced. Peripheral glimpses of the fragmented past that would suddenly float front and center in my vision. An ability I never let myself believe in except when it was happening to me, and it only happened here, in this place my family had lived, in my father's words, since Christ was a corporal. *We've lived here since Christ was a Corporal*, I say to Ashley, and she smiles; it is a term, she tells me later, she has heard her father use.

An empty, dusty bottle of Yoohoo in the stern of the Amish skiff fastens my eyes back to the present, floods me with a sense of relief that the Amish kids are really there, really here, really now.

"You kids were made for each other," I assure the pair. They nod at me.

Here you go, Lady Ashes, Dennis says, passing a joint to her. She draws in the smoke, exhales, hands it to me and I put my lips where her lips were. We are both drunk, but not that much, and in the back seat of Dennis's Camry, the warm skin of her arm against mine, her hip pressed against mine, she smiles and presses in harder and when our eyes meet there is the hint of a promise between us that we both know is as delicate as a strand in a spider web bowed up in a breeze. Later Ashley would say it was only because of what I'd said about fathers and she was a soldier's daughter and we were talking about the war and it was Dennis's last night before the Marines that she had sat with me, and then, when Bledsoe's closed, went with us to the Point. As if Dennis leaving for the war gave us a crazy kind of permission. As if instead of Dennis it was me acting out the cliché of grabbing at the quick of life before descending into the fire.

I turn the kayak into a slot in the saw grass, follow it back into forested country, gliding through a seemingly impassable curtain of reeds that I know is just a fringe. In the growing dusk I see my paddle trail a thread of phosphorescence in the water. I glide forward. The Camry barely stops when Dennis is out of the door whooping and running zigzag down a bluff over the river. By the time we catch up with him, he is already bare-assed and splashing in the water. *Ain't he beautiful*, Ruth chuckles, and runs down to join him. Ashley and I sit in the sand at the foot of the large concrete cross that marks the place the first colonists landed and I tell her inanely how they were welcomed warmly by the Piscataway Indians who thought to stick these hapless newcomers here between themselves and their Susquehannock enemies and she says yes, yes, she knows, and we hear Dennis and Ruth splashing in the river and we smoke again and we both know we are getting high not to lose inhibitions but to give us the excuse that we had done so. The cross stands ghostly, seemingly insubstantial in the night mist hovering over the river and I lean over to her or she leans over to me and we kiss and later, minutes or hours later, Ashley grins the same to-hell-with-it way she had before she'd jumped to our table in Bledsoe's and we go into the river, shifting, crystalline wisps of that mist weaving around and over us, beading on our bodies, sometimes parting and letting the full moon shine through to lay shifting, silvery scales on the black water. Her body rising out of that water to me, skin streaked with glows of phosphorescence and she laughs at the sight of me, at how much I want her, nothing minor there, she says, and when we come together I feel an estuarine blend of sensations I try to memorize even as they slip past: the cold of that river on my skin and the warmth inside her and the current pushing at our legs as she shudders and comes back to herself and pushes me away and we stand laughing, like delighted children, watching a luminescent cloud pulse out of me, ignited by the phosphorescence that always waits like ghosts in that dark water.

I push the bow of the kayak up a few inches onto the bank, and then get out and pull it to shore. Little has changed since the last time I was here. The pin oak stands in a hushed clearing, which is only about fifty yards from the Wheelers' house, set back against the forest. The oak is probably a hundred feet tall, and so thick two adults could not have wrapped their extended arms around it. It is a presence. Dennis and

Tuyết had first taken me here when I was ten years old, the memory, like all my memories this Memorial Day, a palimpsest over the geography in front of my eyes now, past borne into borderless present. Shaded by the tree is a small, grass-covered hillock, about fifteen feet long and five feet high, swelling strangely out of otherwise flat ground; it is, according to Emmett Wheeler, a Native American burial mound. We had accepted his assessment when we were kids because we wanted it to be true; even at ten years old we recognized wishful thinking. But over the years we'd become more certain that he was correct, as we found buried arrowheads and faint cryptic symbols carved into the trunk of the tree, spirals and circles and squares, stretched out and their lines distorted by the tree's growth. Emmett had refused to report the site to the archaeologists at the college; he would not have, he said, whoever was buried there disturbed. One of the few times I saw him and Xuân Wheeler truly angry was when the three of us decided to dig into the mound, using our bare hands. I had gotten deep enough to close my hand around something smooth and long and narrow that could have been a bone or a stick, when they caught us at it. Emmett screamed. But it was the tight-lipped expression on Xuân Wheeler's face, her silent rage, the slight tremble in her hands, that stopped us cold, an expression I had never taken as literal until that moment. A chill went through my blood. Tuyết began to cry.

But Dennis, staring at his mother, just grinned. *Man*, he said, patting the mound, *when I die, this is the place.*

Said as a joke, a way to annoy his mother, I had thought. He loved to tease her, and—most of the time—she loved being teased by him. But over the years, he had repeated that request whenever we came here, the mound and the tree always the end point for all our games, though Tuyết stopped coming with us after that day. The last time he said it to me was after boot camp and just before he was deployed, the two of us drinking cans of Old Boh beer and ceremonially tossing the cans onto the mound, our backs against the tree. It was a promise that of course I could not fulfill. Per the Wheeler family tradition, half his ashes had been interred at St. Inigoes Church and the rest scattered over the river. And even then, I wasn't sure if he was being serious or just being Dennis, presenting me with a dramatic last request before the war, an ironic acknowledgement of our shared vocabulary from the war movies that informed our childhood and that he was going to act out with his own life. Dennis the Menace.

I have brought a small knapsack with me. I unsling it at the base of the tree and draw out a small, blue tablecloth. I spread it between two knotted roots that disappear underground for a few feet and then muscle up out of the earth again as they reach the burial mound. I reach back into the knapsack and pull out the rest of the objects I've brought: a framed photo of Dennis in his green and gold colored gown at our high school graduation; I'd cropped myself out of the picture. A can of Old Boh beer. Two mandarin oranges and two apples. A Hershey chocolate bar. A small bowl. A hand spade. A small bag of rice. A stack of hell money and a bundle of incense sticks I'd bought from the Asian grocery in town.

I rest the photo against the trunk of the tree, its right edge touching one of those connecting roots, pick up the small bowl and fill it with rice. I place it in front of the photo, and then arrange the fruit and chocolate on one side of the tablecloth, the can of Old Boh on the other.

Growing up, I was always invited to the Wheelers' around mid-July— whenever the fifteenth day of the seventh month in the lunar calendar fell—when Xuân Wheeler performed Tết Trung Nguyên, the Day of Wandering Souls, ceremonies at a table covered with food, fruit, flowers, a small plate covered with coins and dollar bills and smoldering incense sticks, their sweet sharp scent diffusing into the air, mixing with and sharpening the heavy scent of the bougainvillea she'd planted around the house. The table was set outside. It was the custom to feed the hungry ghosts who were said to wander the earth that day. But wise not to bring them into your house. There were hundreds of thousands of wandering souls left from the war, Emmett Wheeler had told us, the Vietnamese soldiers missing in action or civilians killed with no place nor family to give them rest, all doomed to roam and starve because their remains were never recovered and buried in ancestral ground. Xuân Wheeler's brother was one of them, Emmett once told us; it was his name that had been given to Dennis, yet for some reason was never to be spoken. The part of the ceremony we three kids liked best was its ending, when Xuân and Emmett would toss the food and money on the table at us, and we would, per the custom, fight each other for it. Enthusiastically. Having grown up Catholic, I liked to imagine being in church and watching parishioners punch each other out as they scrambled for the wafer. This is my body, fight for it. We would wait anxiously while Xuân Wheeler prayed. Once the incense sticks burned down, she would kneel, her hands in front of her chest, bowing until her forehead touched the ground, weeping for her brother, burning a stack of hell money to send to him. But as soon as she looked up and spotted us, she would beam, her face transforming instantly. She would hold up the money plate and start by flinging the coins and bills at us, and then start pelting us with sugar cane, oranges, and chocolate bars. We grabbed at the offerings, punching, pushing, screeching with excitement while she and Emmett Wheeler laughed their asses off. Welcome to VC Halloween, Dennis would always whisper to me, at some point.

I try now to remember and imitate what I would see Xuân Wheeler do as she prayed at that table for lost souls.

I unwrap and light the incense, holding the bundle in one hand and fanning the flame with the other. Pressing the incense between both palms, I close my eyes and slowly bring it up to my forehead and then down again, three times. *The only way, my friend, to escape the legend, is to make your own legend.* I stick the bottoms of the incense sticks into the bowl. I am culturally appropriating like hell, and probably offending both sundry Vietnamese hungry ghosts and whatever Native American spirits rest in that mound. Dennis was not a wandering soul. Not technically. His remains had been returned and commemorated. The ghost I was bringing here was the ghost of our childhood. Dennis would understand. We made things our own. We were our own country. What I always took and treasured from being invited yearly to that wandering souls ceremony was the same gratitude I had felt when Dennis and Tuyết sealed me to themselves by bringing me here, to this secret and sacred place. It is the same way I felt when Dennis told me his secret name.

I watch as the incense sticks burn down, their long fingers transmuted into fragile ash replicas of their original form. A breeze picks up the ash and scatters it.

PREVIOUS PUBLICATION VENUES (IN CHRONOLOGICAL ORDER)

"The Vietnamese Elections," "Medevac," "Search and Destroy," "Extract," in *Free Fire Zone: Short Stories by Vietnam Veterans*, edited by Wayne Karlin, Basil T. Paquet, and Larry Rottmann. New York: First Casualty Press/McGraw-Hill, 1973. "Search and Destroy" also anthologized in *Short Fiction: Classic and Contemporary*, 4th edition, edited by Charles Bohner. Hoboken, NJ: Prentice Hall, 1999.

"Moratorium," in *Swords into Ploughshares: A "Home Front" Anthology*. Burning Cities Press, 1991. Also anthologized in *The Vietnam War in American Stores, Songs, and Poems*, edited by Bruce Franklin. Bedford Books, 1995.

"Nesting," first published as "Payments," in *Prairie Schooner* 69, no. 2 (Summer 1995) and included in *Prisoners: A Novel*, Curbstone Press/Northwestern University Press, 1998.

"The Last VC," in *Vietnam Generation*, August 1992. Also anthologized in *The Vietnam War in American Stores, Songs, and Poems*, edited by Bruce Franklin. Bedford Books, 1995 , and included in *Prisoners: A Novel*, Curbstone Press/Northwestern University Press, 1998.

"Lizard Wine," in *Prairie Schooner* 71, no. 4 (Winter 1997). Also included in *Prisoners: A Novel*, Curbstone Press/Northwestern University Press, 1998.

"American Grass," in *Crab Orchard Review* (Winter 1998). Also included in *War Movies*, Curbstone Press/Northwestern University Press, 1998.

"The Twenty-Fifth Platoon," in *North American Review* 288, no. 2 (March–April 2003).

"The American Reader," in *War, Literature & the Arts* 16, nos. 1–2 (2004). Translation published simultaneously in *Tuổi Trẻ-Youth Magazine*, Hồ Chí Minh City.

"Our Fathers' Wars," in *Gargoyle*/Paycock Press (Fall 2012).

"That Minute," first published as "That Minute: Jacksonville, North Carolina, 1965," in *Gargoyle*/Paycock Press (Spring 2015).

"The Serpent," in *Manoa: A Pacific Journal of International Writing* 31, no. 2 (Fall 2019).

"The War on Terror," in *Gargoyle*/Paycock Press 73 (Winter 2021).

"Memorial Days," in *Dark Mountain, #18* (UK), October 2020. To be published in *Wilderness Tales: 40 Short Stories about the North American Wild*, edited by Diane Fuss. New York: Alfred A. Knopf, 2023.

ABOUT THE AUTHOR

WAYNE KARLIN'S NOVELS INCLUDE *CROSSOVER, LOST Armies, The Extras, Us, Prisoners, The Wished-For Country, Marble Mountain*, and *A Wolf by the Ears*. His nonfiction works are *Rumors and Stones: A Journey, War Movies: Scenes and Out-takes*, and *Wandering Souls: Journeys with the Dead and the Living in Viet Nam*. As co-editor or contributor, he has published *Free Fire Zone: Short Fiction by Vietnam Veterans* (with Basil T. Paquet and Larry Rottmann), *The Other Side of Heaven: Postwar Fiction by Vietnamese and American Writers* (with Lê Minh Khuê and Trường Vũ), *Truyện Ngắn Mỹ Đường Đại* (*Contemporary American Short Stories*) (with Hồ Anh Thái), and *Love After War: Contemporary Fiction from Vietnam* (with Hồ Anh Thái). He has received two Fellowships from the National Endowment for the Arts, the Paterson Prize in Fiction, the Vietnam Veterans of American Excellence in Arts Award, and the Juniper Prize for Fiction.

www.ingramcontent.com/pod-product-compliance
Lightning Source LLC
Chambersburg PA
CBHW031107020726
47495CB00007B/2083